"Hey, baby." His tone was low and intimate—just for her.

She slid her right hand around the back of his neck and took the last step that separated them. Her body melded with his like putty, molding itself to the hard lines, from the broad expanse of his chest to his muscular thighs.

Mia tilted her head slightly upward and brought her mouth to his.

Steven groaned deep in his throat when the softness of her lips connected with his. He maneuvered her so that her back was against the frame of the archway to the kitchen.

The sweetness of her tongue set off a firestorm in his gut. His erection was electrifying and so suddenly powerful that the world receded and an uncontrolled need took its place.

Her long, slender fingers grazed along his body, stoking the growing fire of desire.

Books by Donna Hill

Kimani Romance

Love Becomes Her
If I Were Your Woman
After Dark
Sex and Lies
Seduction and Lies
Temptation and Lies

DONNA HILL

began writing novels in 1990. Since then, she has had more than forty books published, including full-length novels and novellas. Two of her novels and one novella were adapted for television. She has won numerous awards for her body of work. Donna is also the editor of five novels, two of which were nominated for awards. She easily moves from romance to erotica, horror, comedy and women's fiction. She was the first recipient of the Trailblazer Award, and currently teaches writing at the Frederick Douglass Creative Arts Center. Donna lives in Brooklyn with her family. Visit her Web site at www.donnahill.com.

TEMPTATION AND LIES

DONNA HILL

ESSENCE BESTSELLING AUTHOR

KIMANI
ROMANCE

I want to thank my readers who have
continued to support me for the past 18 years!!!!
I love ya.

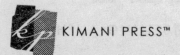 KIMANI PRESS™

ISBN-13: 978-0-373-86100-2
ISBN-10:   0-373-86100-1

TEMPTATION AND LIES

Copyright © 2009 by Donna Hill

www.kimanipress.com

Printed in U.S.A.

Dear Reader,

First and foremost I want to thank the incredible readers and book clubs who have made the TLC series so successful. I appreciate each and every one of you and I plan to keep the stories coming.

I do hope you enjoy this latest installment of the TLC series. I'm having a ball "ripping my stories from the headlines" and dumping them in the laps of my characters.

So far you should have met Savannah from *Sex and Lies* and then Danielle in *Seduction and Lies,* and now I proudly wish to introduce Mia Turner, who will take center stage. I do believe this story is my favorite. Mia is quirky, sexy, smart and in a hot mess of trouble— trapped between two men, a twisted assignment and confusion of the heart! But of course she will have her girls by her side along with a brand-new friend, Ashley Temple.

Be on the lookout for *Scandals and Lies,* coming very soon.

In the meantime, sit back, get a cup of something cold and get to reading! LOL. I'd love to hear what you think. Send me a note to writerdoh@aol.com.

Until we meet again, happy reading!

Donna

omelet that she painstakingly prepared every morning.

Chapter 1

The October sun peeked through the slats in the vertical blinds, throwing a soft glow across the state-of-the-art kitchen. Mia Turner loved to cook and considered herself something of a gourmet chef, always willing to try new recipes. And she firmly believed that a good meal opened and soothed the soul. The best conversations, confessions and gossip could be had over a good meal.

With her piping-hot mug of imported Turkish coffee on the left, her sparkling pearl-handle .22 on the right, she snapped open the *Daily News* and immediately turned to Page Six. She circled several high-profile items about celebs and business tycoons spotted in and around the Big Apple as she sipped her coffee. The smooth blend had been a gift from one of her grateful clients. She made a note on the pad next to her saucer to call Paul Han and thank him for his "thank you."

Page Six aside, she turned her attention to the egg-white omelet that she painstakingly prepared every morning. It was

stuffed with mushrooms, tomatoes, green peppers and ched-
dar cheese. She took a forkful and sighed with pleasure.

There were two things that were paramount in Mia's life:
great food and paying clients. Well, three things—order, too.
No, make that four—Steven.

The last item on her must-have list made her smile and she
thought about the incredible lovemaking session they'd had
just that morning, in this very chair. She wiggled her plump
bottom as images of her and Steven played behind her partially closed lids.

Her best friends, Savannah Fields and Danielle Holloway,
teased her about her neurotic obsessions, but they had to agree
that Steven Long was certainly worth being obsessed about.

Mia was the last of the trio to find someone special in her
life. Savannah and Blake had been married for seven years
and had just had their first child—Mikayla—the most
gorgeous baby girl the world had ever seen. And Danielle had
finally allowed her heart to open and let Nick Mateo in, and
they were now living together and engaged!

For a while Mia believed she'd always be the fifth wheel,
until she actually took a second look at Steven Long.

They'd known each other casually for years: Blake and
Steven were best friends and business partners at their architecture and development company.

But it wasn't until Mia had hosted a party at her house
about ten months earlier that they actually saw each other as
more than "the best friend of their best friend."

Since that night, Mia and Steven had been pretty much in-
separable, only allowing the pressing business of their respective livelihoods to keep them apart.

Mia closed her paper, finished off her omelet and washed
it down with the last of her coffee.

She took her dishes to the sink, rinsed then placed them
in the dishwasher.

This part of her morning ritual completed, she took her gun from the table and walked the short hallway that led from the front of the two-bedroom condo to the back where the master bedroom and reconverted second bedroom were located.

She and Steven used that second bedroom as their combined office, so she would never risk him discovering the contents of her "kit," as Danielle's lover Nick had done.

A minor disaster like that would take more explaining than she was willing to do. So being the orderly and forward-thinking type-A personality that she was, Mia had cut out a little panel behind the top shelf of her clothes closet, hidden behind boxes of very expensive shoes.

She removed the panel and pulled out her TLC "beauty kit." Mia smiled as she ran her hand across the smooth pink leather carrying case with the TLC logo emblazoned across the front.

Taking the case to the bed, she turned the latch to review the contents: burglary tools, computer-scanning disk, listening and recording devices, chloroform and a fingerprint dusting kit and, of course, the container that held the bath beads that were actually specially designed tranquilizer bullets for her .22. All the contents were ingeniously camouflaged as bath oil, body lotions, eye shadows, blush, perfumes and lipsticks. She smiled.

Reassured that everything was in order and accounted for, she lifted the top tray and replaced the gun in its cutout compartment below. She knew it was risky to take the gun out each morning after Steven had left for work, but the thrill of seeing it right next to her, where she could admire and stroke it—even though it only held tranquilizer bullets—still gave her a rush.

Mia had become an official member of the Cartel seven months earlier, although she'd been a fringe member since Savannah's first case a little more than a year ago, which turned up an ugly land deal that would have destroyed an ancient African burial ground right in downtown Brooklyn.

As the owner and CEO of MT Management, Mia's schedule, though hectic, was her own. That flexibility lent itself to her sideline as an undercover operative for TLC.

Mia returned her kit to its hiding place and checked the time. Jean Wallington-Armstrong, the head of the Cartel, had asked Mia to come to the Harlem brownstone to discuss a new assignment that Jean felt Mia was perfect for.

From there it would be off to her real job—the one she could tell everyone about, she thought with a smile.

Event management was the perfect occupation for Mia. It gave her the opportunity to arrange every aspect of an event, down to the most mundane detail, and she loved every minute of it.

Ever since she was a little girl, growing up in Bedford-Stuyvesant in Brooklyn, she'd had a knack for arranging things. As a preschooler she had a precise time and location for all her doll tea parties and all the accessories had to match and be placed "just so" on the tiny pink plastic table.

The most traumatic incident in her young life was when she went to place the teacups on the saucers and discovered that one of the handles was broken and there were no more in her collection that matched. "You see, the tablecloth, paper napkins and the dolls' outfits were all color-coordinated," she'd explained to Savannah and Danielle many years later, who'd both given her sympathetic looks.

She'd become so hysterical that her mother had to promise to replace the entire set the following day. Mia was only five at the time, and her obsession with detail and order only grew and crystallized as she got older.

Of course, now she didn't collapse into tears and fits when things went awry, but her entire demeanor would become one tightly wound band of tension that was terribly uncomfortable to be around.

That aside, Mia Turner was your everyday, ordinary kind of woman unless, of course, you counted her other life.

She squinted at her appearance in the oval hall mirror. Her smooth, shoulder-length hair haloed her face in soft waves. The slight touches of makeup—bronze lip gloss, mascara and a little powder to keep the shine off her nose—kept her lovely features from being overshadowed. She cinched the belt on her knee-length dress, took her coat and purse and headed out, checking the locks three times before she felt comfortable.

Twenty minutes later she pulled onto 135th Street in Harlem. She parked her midnight-blue Lexus two doors down from the brownstone. The luxury car was a recent present to herself for having achieved a stellar year of profits from her business. In these tight economic times, everyone was cutting back, but her business continued to flourish. Big business, celebrities and the well-off were always having conventions or hosting parties to sell something, impress others or remind everyone else how important they were, and MT Management was the one they invariably called.

Mia slid off her glasses and tucked them into her purse. She was terribly nearsighted but refused to wear her glasses in public and was adamant against "sticking something in her eyes" as she put it, referring to contact lenses. So vanity won out and she went through life squinting, which often gave her a severe appearance that was totally contrary to her open and warm personality. In business, however, it often worked to her advantage: in her dealings and negotiations, her steely gaze gave the impression of a no-nonsense businesswoman.

She gathered her purse and hopped out, her chocolate-colored Milano ankle boots hitting the pavement with a soft pop.

She grabbed her ecru-colored swing coat from the hook in the back of the car and quickly slipped it on. Although it was early October and the sun was high in the sky, the weather had already begun to grow cool.

Setting the alarm on the car, she headed to the brownstone and rang the bottom bell.

Within moments, Claudia, Savannah's mother, came to the door.

"Hello, darling," Claudia greeted her, enveloping Mia in a warm hug. The soft scent of Chanel floated around her.

Claudia Martin was in her early sixties, but she didn't look a day over forty-five. Class and style always exuded from Claudia. She kept her auburn-tinted hair in a fierce cut that mimicked the early Halle Berry look. Her cinnamon complexion was flawless and she rarely wore much makeup, save for a dash of lipstick and mascara to accentuate her incredible hazel eyes. St. John was her designer of choice and she wore it well.

Claudia had been a member of TLC for several years and had recruited her daughter, Savannah. And all those years that Mia, Savannah and Danielle had seen Claudia toting around her TLC carryall and saying she was going to meetings, they'd always believed what she told them: that she was selling beauty products. Ha!

The joke between them, now that Savannah had a daughter of her own, would be that she would recruit little Mikayla when she came of age. Knowing her already feisty infant, Savannah had said Mikayla would probably launch her own division of TLC Tots!

"Looking good as always, Claudia. Bernard must be treating you well. You're glowing."

Claudia laughed lightly. "That he does, my dear. Nothing like a good man to get the kinks out." She winked at Mia and walked inside.

"Have you two finally set a date?"

"Actually, I wanted to talk to you about that." She clasped Mia's arm and her diamond ring flashed in the late-morning light. "Now that Savannah had the baby and can fit into something 'fabulous,' as she said, we wanted a December wedding. Do you think you can put something together in time?"

Mia stopped short, propped her hand on her hip and gave Claudia a look of mild reprimand. "Claudia, this is me. If you said your wedding was this afternoon and you wanted it in Paris, I would make it happen. It's what I do."

Claudia laughed in response. "Chile, what was I thinking? Go on," she said, still chuckling. "Jean is upstairs in her office."

"We'll make an appointment to talk," she promised before heading off.

Mia went up the stairs and down the "hall of fame" as it had been dubbed. The walls on either side were lined with portraits of all the Cartel members who had been affiliated for at least a year and had successfully completed their assignments. She smiled as she spotted Savannah's photo and then two photos down was one of Danielle. Claudia's was at the beginning of the row, right next to Jean. Mia drew in a breath of resolve. One day soon her photo would grace the hall of fame, too.

Mia knocked lightly on the closed door.

"Come in." Jean looked up from her computer screen when Mia entered. "Have a seat. I'll be right with you."

Mia did as instructed, taking in the room while she waited. As with all of the brownstones in Harlem and in Brooklyn— which had not been cut up or converted—the rooms were enormous; *grand* would be a better word. Vaulted ceilings, crystal chandeliers, parquet floors, mahogany sliding doors, massive mantelpieces, stained-glass windows and working fireplaces. Some even had the claw-foot bathtubs and original porcelain sconces.

She'd grown up in a brownstone on Putnam Avenue in Brooklyn. Not quite as big as this one, but large enough. So any time she came here she felt right at home.

Mia crossed her legs.

"Thank you for coming," Jean began, bypassing any pleasantries.

Mia merely nodded, knowing from experience that Jean wasn't one for chitchat.

"I have an assignment that is perfect for you, especially with the business that you're in."

Jean took a sealed manila envelope from her desk drawer. "All the details are inside. I'll briefly give you some background. This was handed to me from a personal contact at the FBI. There are some extremely high-profile individuals involved and before the lid gets blown off, they need to be absolutely sure." She cleared her throat and removed her red-framed glasses, setting them gently down on the desktop. "There is a major, very elite, very exclusive escort service operating in New York City. Although that's nothing new, what is new is that it appears to be run by Avante Enterprises. You need to find a way to get inside the organization, and get the evidence that the Feds need to shut it down."

For an instant, Mia couldn't move. She hoped that Jean couldn't read the distress on her face, or hear the escalated pounding of her heart. Avante Enterprises had been one of her clients, and several years ago she'd broken a cardinal rule and had a short but fiery affair with its CEO, Michael Burke.

Chapter 2

Mia managed to get through the rest of the briefing without screaming. When she got behind the wheel of her Lexus, she wasn't quite certain she'd heard anything Jean had said after she'd dropped her Michael Burke bombshell.

By rote she turned the key in the ignition. The engine purred to life, along with the sounds of Marvin Gaye's classic, "What's Going On?"

That was the question of the day, she mused. She put on her glasses, drew in a long steadying breath and slowly pulled off in the early-afternoon traffic.

In the privacy of her business office, a ground-floor rental in SoHo, Mia closed and locked the door on the off chance that her new assistant, Ashley Temple, might decide to burst in—as she was prone to do—to update her on the latest TMZ news (a celebrity online and off-line news outlet). She was relieved that Ashley wasn't up front when she came in and she was able to get to her office undetected, at least for the time being.

Mia depressed the Do Not Disturb button on her phone, then removed the manila envelope from her purse.

She placed it on the desk and stared at the innocuous-looking envelope. It looked like millions of others, but she knew better. The contents had the potential to turn her life inside out.

The affair between her and Michael had been discreet. No one knew about it, especially within the business circles they traveled in. Not even Savannah or Danielle had any idea that anything had transpired. They'd always believed that she simply hadn't found the right man and, until she'd met Michael, she hadn't.

When they broke up, it was a long three years before she started intermittently dating. But she'd never found anyone who could measure up—until Steven Long.

Mia ran her manicured finger across the smooth surface of the envelope.

If she broke the seal and opened it, there was no turning back. She'd have to carry out the assignment. Her type-A personality wouldn't allow her to give up or turn the reins over to someone else.

Drawing in a long breath, she exhaled her doubts and trepidations and broke the seal.

The documents detailed Michael's rise up the business ranks to eventually running his own management company. He was considered one of the best in the management consulting business.

Her pulse pounded in her temples when she scrolled down to review his personal information.

Marital Status: Divorced

Reflexively, she gripped the pages tighter between her fingers. Her heart thumped as her breathing shortened.

Divorced. He was free. At least on paper.

He was married when they'd met. Guilt had riddled her each time they'd made love until her conscience had no longer allowed her to do that to another woman. Michael had literally begged her not to leave him. He'd promised to get a divorce—just give me some time, he'd said.

But time and promises were things she could not depend on, nor did she want to.

"I can't do this anymore, Michael," she recalled saying to him, the agony of speaking the words making her voice paper thin, sounding weak and without conviction.

He turned onto his side. His dark brown eyes moved slowly along her face. His thumb brushed across her bottom lip. "Do what?" he asked, his voice husky and taunting. "This?" His large hand slid between her damp thighs and gently caressed her there.

Mia drew in a sharp breath as the powerful sensations rippled through her.

"Michael…" Her hips arched. She gripped his shoulders and he rose above her, bracing his weight on his forearms.

"I love you so much, Mia," he said on a ragged breath as he pushed slowly inside her.

Mia wrapped her body and her heart around him, giving him all of her because she knew that this could never happen again.

And it didn't.

Mia ran her hand along the length of her hair and for a moment shut her eyes, wishing the images of the past away.

She looked down and read further. Michael had been under surveillance for a while. He'd come under suspicion during a routine audit of his company's finances. There were several discrepancies, which had apparently been cleared up, but he remained a blip on the radar screen.

Apparently, deposits of three to five thousand dollars were routinely placed in one of his secondary accounts, then were quickly transferred to an offshore account in the Cayman Islands.

The more she read, the more ill she became.

The Michael Burke she knew was ambitious, and he could be manipulative if it would land him an account. But this man on paper was not the man she remembered and had once loved.

She closed the folder and knew that shortly the ink would disappear, as if the damning words had never existed.

The knock on her door snapped her to attention. She shoved the envelope into her desk drawer, removed her glasses and went to unlock the door.

"Hi. Come in."

Ashley's updated Angela Davis fro bounced in a cinnamon-brown halo around her openly expressive face.

Every time she looked at Ashley, Mia thought of a highly energetic, inquisitive child, even though Ashley was easily in her early thirties.

Ashley was a godsend after Mia lost her last assistant to marriage and happily ever after. Ashley was bright, totally efficient and loved the event-planning business. She was so good, in fact, that Mia had given Ashley two of her own accounts to manage, and her clients loved her.

"Hey, boss," Ashley greeted her, her warm brown eyes sparkling, as always. Her deep dimples flashed.

"What's up?"

"A couple of calls that I thought you'd want to handle personally." She handed Mia a slip of the company's teal-colored message paper.

They walked toward the small circular table in the far corner of the office and sat down.

Mia squinted at the words on the page until they came into focus. "Sahara Club?" she asked.

Ashley read from a sheet in her hand detailing all the particulars about the Sahara Club, which catered to married couples who wanted to plan quick romantic getaways. The club management wanted to put together an event to promote their business, inviting previous guests to give testimonials about their experience.

Mia's brows rose as she listened.

"I did an Internet search on them," Ashley offered in response to the question that hovered on Mia's lips. She handed over her research material. "I also have a short list of some of their clients. I can have them checked, if you want."

Mia took the notes and briefly scanned them, the words blurry around the edges.

"This one is for the grand opening of a boutique in Tribeca," she went on reading her second set of notes. "They want something really upscale. They'd like to come in and talk with you. Should I schedule it?"

"Why don't you take that one?" Mia said absently. "I'll sit in on the initial meeting if you need me, but I think you can handle it."

"No problem." She paused a moment. "Are you okay? You seem really out of it."

In the six months that Ashley had worked for Mia, they'd grown rather close, sharing stories and giving each other advice on things like clothes, cars, best deals, politics, religion. Mia had even invited Ashley to join her, Savannah and Danielle for their weekly girls' brunch at their favorite hangout, The Shop. Over time Mia had grown to respect Ashley's judgment and clearheaded opinions, which she often sought out. But her current dilemma she could not share.

"I'm fine. Just a little headache."

Ashley leaned forward. "Maybe if you wore your glasses to read and move around in the world, your head would stop hurting. It's probably eyestrain."

Mia made a face. It was her personal pet peeve. "I'll be fine. I'll take something for it."

Ashley huffed. "Suit yourself." She pushed up from the desk. "I'll give these ladies from the boutique a call and get that set up."

"Thanks."

Alone now, Mia's thoughts reluctantly turned to her most pressing situation: in order to complete her assignment, she was going to have to see Michael again. And she wasn't sure how she was going to handle that.

What she needed was some advice. Savannah was totally out of the question. She was a devout believer in the sanctity of marriage. She'd had her own scare with her husband, Blake, and she didn't look favorably on the "other woman," which is what Mia had been.

Danielle, though much more open-minded, had mellowed since she'd settled down with Nick. And although she might be more understanding, Dani's quick, sharp tongue was not something she wanted to deal with, either.

Those were the reasons why she'd never told her two best friends about what had gone on between her and Michael. It went against everything they believed in. She'd cringe every time the topic of adultery and cheating came up during their chats. She never wanted to disappoint them or see that appalled look in their eyes. She knew they'd demand an explanation as to why, and she wouldn't be able to provide one, because she didn't know why.

Sounds of Ashley singing a very bad rendition of a Mary J. Blige tune drifted to her ears. Mia smiled. Oh, to be carefree, she mused.

Her phone rang.

"MT Management, Mia speaking."

"Hey, baby. Caught you at your desk."

"Hi, sweetie. This is a surprise. To what do I owe the pleasure?"

"I have a couple of hours and I thought I'd swing by and take my favorite girl to a late lunch. If you haven't eaten already."

"I'd love to."

"Great. See you in about twenty minutes."

"Okay." Mia hung up the phone. Spending some time with Steven was just what she needed.

As promised, twenty minutes later, Steven came walking through the door.

Mia's heart skipped a beat when she saw him. She stood and came from behind her desk, her body warming with every step.

"Hi," she whispered as she came to a stop in front of him.

Steven Long was, for lack of a better word, gorgeous. His complexion was the color of polished mahogany, he had a hard square jaw and chocolate-brown eyes with silky brows and lashes to die for.

Two years in a row *Jet* magazine had listed him as one of New York's most eligible bachelors. That was before he'd hooked up with Mia. Now he was off the market—permanently, if Mia had any say in the matter.

His gunmetal gray suit fit every inch of his six-foot frame, and damn if she didn't love a man in a good-looking suit. His pearl-gray shirt and burgundy-and-gray-striped tie set off the suit and his skin to perfection.

Steven snaked his arm around Mia's waist and swept her into a deep, lingering kiss that took her breath away. When he released her, she felt shaken and hot with desire.

"You're going to have to stop by more often," she said, stroking his cheek with the tip of her finger.

He grinned. "If only I could, gorgeous. How's your day been so far?"

Reality slammed into her. Her heart thumped. "Uh, not bad. We may have two more clients."

"That's great. Congrats."

"Good for business, but not great for relationships. It means that I'll be even busier," she said, knowing that in the coming weeks she would need time away from Steven.

He took her hand and massaged the center of her palm in sensuous circular motions that sent shivers running through her.

"If anyone can multitask and make it look like child's play, it's you, babe." He pecked her softly on the lips. "I ain't worried," he said with a grin. "Come on, let's go before we spend all our free time talking about what time we won't have."

"Lead the way."

"How did you manage to get time away from the office?" Mia asked as they were seated in a back booth at Brothers Bistro, a great health-food eatery within walking distance of her office.

"Blake is in the field taking some sketches of the renovation project in Brooklyn. This morning I put the finishing touches on the blueprints for the town houses in D.C. and realized I actually had some breathing room for a change."

It was amazing how far Steven and Blake had come in just over a decade. They'd built their business from a two-man company, working out of a storefront, to one of the major players with a staff of ten, an office in midtown and contracts that were expanding their business from its Manhattan locale to the capital.

"If business keeps growing this way, any midday getaway would be wishful thinking," Steven said.

"Are you and Blake planning to hire more people?"

"We may have to, just to handle the volume. But my fear

is, as I've explained to Blake, at some point the bottom is going to drop out. Builders are going to stop building because no one can afford to buy."

Mia nodded in agreement. She knew all too well the fragility of the current economy and how it had wreaked havoc on countless American businesses, not to mention the thousands who'd lost their homes.

"I don't want to have to hire new people and realize in six months or a year that we have to let them go."

"What does Blake say?"

"You know Blake, Mr. Optimistic. But I think I'm getting him to see my point."

"So what's plan B?"

"Work our asses off," he said with a chuckle.

Mia raised her water glass. "To working our asses off."

As she sat there laughing and talking with the man she loved and who loved her back, she knew that it was only a matter of time before the lies began. And she could only pray that he never found out—not so much about the Cartel, which would be devastating enough—but about her and Michael.

Savannah's censure she could live with. Danielle's sharp tongue she could handle. But the hurt and lack of respect that she knew would be in Steven's eyes would kill her inside. She would do whatever it took to keep that information from him. She'd get through it.

But the true test would come when she saw Michael again for the first time. She knew it would be soon.

Much too soon.

Chapter 3

It had been three days since Mia received her assignment and she had yet to do anything about it. She felt frozen, torn between what she had agreed to do—the oath she'd sworn—and the possible repercussions if she did what was necessary.

"Mia."

She glanced up from the files on her desk and was surprised to see Ashley standing in front of her.

"I…didn't hear you come in," she muttered.

"I know. I knocked three times, but you didn't answer. I've been standing here for a good thirty seconds and you didn't budge. Is everything okay? You've been totally distracted for the past few days. That's so not like you."

Mia sighed heavily and leaned back in her chair. She'd been debating about sharing some of her dilemma with Ashley—an abridged version—in hopes of getting an objective view. But because of the sensitivity of the issue, she'd balked at airing her dirty laundry. But holding it in was driving her crazy.

She was a person of action, one who dealt with issues head-on. This inertia was maddening.

"You want to talk?" Ashley gently nudged. "I'm a pretty good listener," she added with an encouraging smile.

Mia pressed her lips together in thought. Finally, she spoke. "Have you ever been in a situation when an old flame came back into your life?"

"Sure. Why?" She sat down on the chair beside Mia's desk.

"What did you do?"

"Well, we had dinner, talked about old times, the way things were. I spent the night at his place and we woke up the next morning and realized that it was truly over—you can't go back. At least Dave and I couldn't."

"Hmm." Mia's gaze drifted away. Spending the night with Michael was not an option. She couldn't do that to Steven in a million years.

"Is that what's going on?" Ashley tentatively asked.

Mia turned her gaze on Ashley. "Something like that. I'll put it this way, seeing him again is inevitable."

"And you don't know how to handle it."

"It's been a long time," Mia admitted. "But a lot was left unresolved."

"Well, I'd never be one to tell somebody what to do, but the one thing I do know, unless you resolve whatever it is that's eating at you, it will always jump up and get in your way." She smiled softly. "You'll work it out."

Ashley hopped up from her seat. "My bill is in the mail," she teased, drawing a chuckle from Mia. "The meeting with Verve Boutique is still on for noon."

"Right. The ones from Tribeca."

"Yep. They should be here soon."

Mia nodded. "Buzz me when you're ready."

"Sure." She headed for the door then stopped. "Mia…"

"Yes."

"As I said, I don't give advice often, but if I can offer this one piece—just think with your head and not with your heart." She tossed up her hands. "That's it." She grinned and sauntered out.

Ashley was right, Mia thought. She was thinking and projecting based on pure emotion and old memories.

Michael was more than over her by now. She was sure he'd moved on and was probably involved with someone else.

She was getting bent out of shape about nothing. What she needed to concentrate on was finding a way to get the information she needed.

That thought was like a knife to the chest. The idea that Michael could be behind an escort service still stunned her. It seemed impossible. But the reality was that people change. And if that adage was true, then Michael Burke was definitely not the man she remembered.

Think with your head.

That's exactly what she was going to start doing. She swiveled her chair toward the flat-screen computer monitor that sat on the right-hand side of her desk. She did a quick search of Avante Enterprises. Within moments a list of choices came up on the screen. She chose the link that opened the company Web site.

Michael's handsome face greeted her and her breath caught in her throat as a flood of memories rushed to the surface. *Think with your head.* She pushed the images back and started taking notes.

Before she knew it, she'd filled three pages and Ashley was buzzing her about their noon appointment. She shoved the notes in her desk. At least she'd done something concrete, she thought, mildly satisfied with herself.

She closed the file, got up from her desk and went to join the ladies in the conference space.

* * *

Felicia and Linda Hall were sisters and the proud owners of Verve. They'd been in business for about a year, but had never had the grand opening that they really wanted. Now, with some experience under their belts and a solid customer base, they thought it was time.

Felicia was the talker of the two, and wasted no time laying out what they wanted: a full weekend with music, entertainment, food and plenty of media coverage, she'd said.

"What kind of budget do you have to work with?" Mia asked.

"Five thousand dollars. Six max," Felicia answered. "But we're really hoping you can do it for four." She flashed a hopeful smile that revealed a tiny gap in her front teeth.

On cue, Ashley and Mia stole a glance at each other. Five would barely cover their expenses, not to mention putting on the event.

Ashley's look clearly said, *It's your decision, but I like them.*

"Why don't I have Ashley put some ideas together for you and what we think is feasible and we'll get back to you with a proposal by the end of the week. How's that?"

The sisters smiled in unison. The gap mirrored on their faces.

Felicia stuck out her hand toward Mia. "Thank you so much." She shook Mia's hand, then did the same with Ashley.

"I really hope you'll consider taking us on," Linda said, the first time she'd spoken since they'd arrived.

Ashley stood. Her notebook pressed against her small breasts. "By the way, I meant to ask, how did you find out about us?"

"Oh, a friend of ours who helped to get our business up and running," Felicia offered.

"Michael Burke," the sisters sang in harmony.

"He recommended you very highly," Felicia added.

Mia held back a yelp of surprise. Her pulse pounded so loudly that the voices faded into the background. She wasn't sure if she'd even said goodbye.

The sound of the front door closing snapped her to attention. She was alone in the conference room.

Recommended by Michael Burke. Coincidence or just her luck? Manhattan, for all its pomp and circumstance and worldwide notoriety, was nothing more than an island jampacked with people and buildings. Sooner or later paths were bound to cross.

So he hadn't forgotten about her and even thought enough of her to recommend a possible client. She didn't know if that was a good or a bad thing, but it *was* one thing—the opening that she needed.

Chapter 4

Michael Burke tugged off his suit jacket and tossed it on the back of the couch before heading across the gleaming wood floor of his condo to the minibar on the far side of the living room.

He took out a bottle of brandy and poured a short tumbler full—no ice. It was a habit he'd picked up over the past few years. The years after his divorce, the years after Mia.

He took a long swallow, closed his eyes and let the smooth, warm liquid work its way down and hopefully soothe the constant ache that had found a home in the center of his gut.

Absently, he put the glass on the top of the bar counter and went to the window. Lights flickered in apartment windows and in offices inhabited by the lone employee working overtime to impress the boss.

Michael braced his palm against the frame of the window. The sky suddenly lit up, followed by a loud crack of thunder.

The rain would come soon, Michael thought. On nights

like this, when he could get away, he remembered walking through the city with Mia, laughing and hugging as they darted under the eaves of buildings and into doorways, stealing kisses like teenagers.

His jaw clenched reflexively. He had many memories of Mia. But the one that stood out in his mind was the day she walked out of his life.

They'd spent a glorious night together at the Hilton on Avenue of the Americas. His wife, Christine, was visiting her mother in Philadelphia, her childhood home. She'd been gone for a week and was due back the following day. Michael intended to make the most of his last night of freedom.

"I can't do this," she'd said. He remembered teasing her about what she'd meant before making love to her, pouring his heart and soul into her.

When he awoke the next morning she was gone. He called and called. He went to her apartment and got no answer. Her neighbors said they hadn't seen her.

She was working for a small management company at the time, and when he inquired about her, he was informed that she'd taken a leave of absence.

For weeks afterward, he couldn't sleep, and he barely ate. Every time his phone rang, he knew it would be Mia, but it never was.

Then about three months later a letter came to his office, no return address.

Dear Michael,
    I know I took the coward's way out. But if I didn't I would have never found the strength to leave you.
    No matter what it is that we feel for each other, it was wrong. We were wrong. And if I could do that to another woman, then what kind of woman did that make me?

I hurt. Every day I hurt. But I know in time it will get better. And you will find a way to be the husband Christine deserves.

I wish you all good things, my love, now and always.

Please don't try to contact me. It's best for all of us.
Mia

He still had that letter. He'd kept it all these years. Memorized every line. He would recite it to himself whenever the overwhelming urge to call or see her would consume him.

Most ironic, less than a year after Mia walked out of his life, Christine filed for divorce. She'd found someone else.

He supposed it was what he'd deserved, and he'd agreed to the divorce uncontested.

Michael turned away from the window, just as the rain began to fall. He was a free man now, a wealthy man who could have whomever and whatever he wanted. He wanted Mia Turner. And he was going to have her, no matter how long it took or what it took to achieve his goal. He'd honored her wishes not to contact her, until now.

He picked up the remnants of his drink and finished it off. It was just a matter of time, he thought as the golden-brown liquid heated his insides. A matter of time.

"Whew, it's pouring out there," Steven muttered, shaking himself off as he crossed the threshold of the apartment that he and Mia shared.

He'd given up his tiny one-bedroom apartment when he and Mia decided that they wanted to be with each other exclusively. That was six months ago, and he hadn't regretted a day of it.

He'd often envied the stability of Blake and Savannah's marriage, although he would never admit that to Blake, even though they were best friends. Blake and Savannah were a team and the union had grounded and matured Blake in a way that nothing else had. Savannah and now their new baby were his life. And the business that he and Blake had built from the ground up, which had been his number-one priority, now took second place to his wife and daughter.

Steven had often teased Blake about how square he'd become since his marriage: no more hanging out with the fellas, dating, chasing women, or even talking about them. Steven couldn't imagine himself with the same woman day in and day out—tied down. The thought often chilled him. Until he met Mia. She turned his world on its ear and he was still pleasantly reeling from the aftershocks. Never in his wildest imaginings did he think he'd be looking forward to coming home to his woman at night.

He shook his head in wonder as he dropped his umbrella in the stand by the door.

Sounds of the evening news drifted from the television set in the living room, mixed with the tantalizing aromas of something distinctly Italian.

Steven grinned. Mia sure knew the way to her man's heart—knockout sex and a mouthwatering meal.

Mia poked her head out from the archway leading to the kitchen. Her face was scrubbed clean of makeup and her skin seemed to glow. Her hair was pulled up into a ponytail, revealing the soft angles of her brown sugar-toned face. She greeted him with one of her heart-stopping smiles. God, he loved her.

Steven moved in her direction until he was right next to her. His gray-green eyes moved like a trained masseur's stroke across her face.

"Hey, baby." His tone was low and very intimate—just for her.

She slid her right hand around the back of his neck and took the last step that separated them. Her body melded with his like putty, molding itself to the hard lines of his from the broad expanse of his chest to his muscular thighs.

Mia tilted her head slightly upward and brought her mouth to his.

Steven groaned deep in his throat when the softness of her lips connected with his. He maneuvered her so that her back was against the frame of the archway to the kitchen.

The sweetness of her tongue set off a firestorm in his gut. His erection was electrifying and so suddenly powerful that the world receded and an uncontrolled need took its place.

Her long, slender fingers grazed along his body, stoking the growing fire of desire. She reached up and pushed down the fragile spaghetti straps of her thin top and tugged it down, exposing her bare breasts.

Steven nearly hollered. Instead, he feasted on one then the other, as Mia's short nails dug into his shoulder blades and her whispers of "Yes, yes, yes," rose in concert with the thunder that boomed in the night.

He dropped to his knees, pulling down her cutoff shorts and pink thong in the process, until he came face-to-face with her hidden treasure. Like a moth to a flame he was drawn to her, taking the tiny pearl between his lips and teasing and stroking it with his tongue until her inner thighs began to tremble and her knees grew weak.

Steven rose, unbuckling his belt and unzipping his pants in one smooth motion, freeing himself, his phallus hard and pulsing. He lifted her off the floor and she wrapped her legs tightly around his waist and locked her arms around his neck.

She was hot and wet when Steven pushed up inside her and he nearly exploded with that first thrust.

Their coupling was hard and fast, the need between them so intense that fulfillment was the one and only goal.

And when it came, their cries of ecstasy rose above the drumroll of thunder and was more brilliant than the lightning that kept silhouetting the Manhattan skyline.

* * *

Mia sat behind the closed doors of her office, reviewing the data that she'd collected on Michael and Avante Enterprises. He was currently the management company for Mercury Entertainment, which groomed and produced new R & B stars. She did a check of the client list and found it to be impressive, to say the least. She recognized more than a few of the names. According to the information that she had, Avante was in the process of planning a major red-carpet event to debut its new artists.

She smiled. She had what she needed. Although Avante oversaw the operations, they subcontracted out all the work.

Mia turned on her shredder and one by one she slid the pages through. Couldn't be too careful.

All night, even after that incredible erotic romp with Steven, her thoughts continued to drift back to Michael and the job at hand. She knew how weak she could be when it came to Michael. She had maintained her strength by staying away from him all these years. That was about to end.

She knew that she was tempting fate by opening a door that would best be left closed. However, she'd sworn an oath to the Cartel: not only would she uphold the tenets of secrecy, but she would execute her assignments to the best of her ability for the ultimate good of society, without regard to personal interest.

Mia believed in the mission of the Cartel to right wrongs and to protect the welfare of the innocent, as an aid to law enforcement. She took it all very seriously, and she could not allow her personal issues to hamper her ability to get the information that she needed on the escort service.

Besides, she was a big girl. She could handle herself with Michael. Plenty of time, space and other people had passed between them—enough to make what she had to do strictly business.

Strictly business, she counseled herself, as she dialed the offices of Avante Enterprises.

"Good morning. My name is Mia Turner, MT Management. I'd like to speak with Mr. Burke."

"Please hold."

Mia squeezed her eyes shut and sucked in a breath. She wondered if the receptionist could hear the uncontrollable pounding of her heart that was surely vibrating through the phone.

Another voice, more controlled, less perky came on the line.

"May I help you?"

"Yes. I'm calling to speak with Mr. Burke."

"Mr. Burke is very busy at the moment. Maybe I can help you."

She hadn't realized that Michael had risen to the point of having two screeners for his calls.

"Perhaps if you let him know that it's Mia Turner…"

There was a moment of deafening silence.

Ms. Control cleared her throat. "He really cannot be disturbed, but I'll be happy to take a message."

Mia's slender neck jerked back. She was about to blurt out, "Say what?" but remembered who she was—a professional.

"Why don't I do this—I'll call him on his cell a bit later. Perhaps he won't be so busy then," she said, playing the power game. Of course, she didn't have Michael's cell-phone number, but this chick didn't know that. "And who am I speaking with?"

"Brenda Forde. I'm Mr. Burke's executive assistant."

I'll just bet you are. "Thanks so much for your help… Brenda." She hung up.

Mia sat back and tugged on her bottom lip with her teeth. She could have left a number for him to call her back, but that would have defeated her purpose of pretending to have the upper hand. Besides, she wasn't quite ready for Michael to have a direct connection to her.

But now that she'd lied and said she'd reach him on his cell phone, she'd have no logical reason to call back.

While she was pondering her next move, Ashley buzzed her on the intercom.

Mia stabbed the flashing red light. "Yes."

"There's a Michael Burke on the line for you."

Mia nearly choked. "Who?" she asked with all the calm she could summon.

"Michael Burke. Could that be the Michael Burke of Avante Enterprises—the one that Felicia and Linda said referred them?"

"I…suppose so." Her heart was galloping at breakneck speed.

"He's on line two."

"Thanks," she managed. "I'll take it."

For several moments she stared at the flashing red light. Would he sound the same? What did he want? How would she respond?

The unanswered questions rushed through her head. Finally she picked up the phone.

"Hello?"

"Mia…"

The deep bass of his voice rolled through her in waves. For an instant nothing stood between them, but then she remembered what she had to do.

"Michael, how are you?"

"Actually, quite well."

Silence. Then they both spoke at once.

"You first," Michael conceded.

"I wanted to thank you for the referral. I must admit I was surprised when they told me it had come from you."

"Why?"

The one-word question was suffused with a melancholy tone. Although it was asking the obvious, the inflection of his voice was asking her for an answer she couldn't give.

"I…had no idea…"

"What, that I've followed your career?"

He had? "Well…yes."

"I have. I know all about your business, that you're doing very well. I have friends who have seen you around the city. They tell me that you're still beautiful," he said softly.

She shut her eyes and a Technicolor image of Michael bloomed behind her lids.

"So now that we've gotten the formalities out of the way, was that the only reason for your call today?"

Mia cleared her throat and tried to clear her mind, but it was pointless.

"Yes. Why else would I call? I mean, it was very generous of you and I wanted to thank you."

"I think you know that I've always wanted the best for…my clients and myself. And that's what you are."

Why couldn't she get her brain to work and her lips to move? She felt like an idiot. Concentrate.

"I took a look at some of the projects that you're working on," she finally said, taking the first step into the land of no return. "And I was wondering if you'd contracted with any-one for the upcoming red-carpet event for Raven, the new R & B artist."

"I have two outfits that I'm considering, but if you wanted to handle it, I can call them off right now."

She laughed nervously. "Just like that?"

"Why not? You are the best at what you do?"

She drew in a breath.

"Why don't we meet and talk about it?"

This was going better than she'd hoped. "Sure, I can come to your office." She needed to get access in order to plant some listening devices and perhaps a small camera.

"I thought we could discuss it over drinks. I can have a car pick you up at your office about six."

"Six? Tonight?"

"No time like the present. You do want the assignment, don't you?"

"I don't even have a proposal prepared."

"We can discuss it when we see each other. Six o'clock. A black Lincoln will be out front. I've got to go. I have a meeting in a few minutes. I'll see you later." He disconnected the call before she could come up with a reason not to.

Slowly, she returned the handset to its cradle. Six o'clock. Absently she glanced up at the clock on the wall. Four hours. She had four hours to prepare to see the man her heart would not let her forget.

There would never be enough time.

Chapter 5

Mia walked to the front of the office. Ashley was just hanging up from a call. She looked at Mia curiously.

"You okay? You look…shaken."

Mia pressed her lips tightly together, as if the action could somehow hold back the words she needed to say. She pulled up a chair next to Ashley's desk and slowly sat down.

"Remember the other day I asked you if an old flame had ever come back into your life?"

"Yeah," she said, drawing out the word into two syllables.

Mia glanced away. "Well, my old love asked me out for drinks."

Ashley's finely arched brows rose. "Oh. Okay. Was this your idea or his?"

"His!" she said much too quickly. The guilt already getting to her.

"Why don't you start at the beginning? Maybe that would help."

The beginning. Yes, she could do that. Perhaps it was time.

Mia looked directly at Ashley. "I've never told this to anyone. No one. Not even Savannah and Danielle," she said with a new pang of guilt for having kept her two best friends in the dark for so long. She drew in a long breath and as she released it, the illicit love affair spilled out on a rough tide of emotion.

Nearly an hour later, Mia blinked back the past and her gaze rested on Ashley, waiting for condemnation, a look of reprimand. Instead, she saw tears welling up in Ashley's eyes.

Ashley sniffed and dabbed at the corner of her almond-shaped eyes with the tip of her index finger. "Wow," she sputtered. "A true-life, tragic love story." She folded her hands together. "And now he's single?"

Mia bobbed her head.

Ashley pressed her hands flat on the desktop and leaned forward. "Do you love Steven?"

The question taunted her, tugged at her heart.

Of course she loved Steven, she told herself again as the black Lincoln navigated in and out of midtown Manhattan rush-hour traffic.

That's what she said to Ashley, who told her simply, "Keep that at the forefront of your thoughts and then when you see Michael everything will fall into place."

Mia certainly hoped so.

The driver gave her no indication where they were going. He'd only told her that Mr. Burke had arranged for dinner.

Dinner! That wasn't the agreement, she'd worried. Drinks were impersonal. Dinner was intimate. It raised this meeting to another level.

When she next looked out the window, she realized that they were leaving the city. She grabbed her glasses from her purse and the directional signs came into focus. The driver had taken the exit to the FDR Drive.

She tapped on the Plexiglas partition. The window slowly whirred downward.

"Yes, Ms. Turner?"

"Where are we going?"

"To dinner."

"You said that already."

"That's all I know, Ms. Turner."

"You must know where you were told to drive," she pressed, trying to control her rising temper, which was being overshadowed by her rising panic.

The partition whirred back into place, cutting off any further communication.

It was just like Michael to dream up something elaborate. But how in the world would she be able to explain what would certainly be a late night to Steven?

Sighing, she settled back against the plush leather. There wasn't much that she could do other than wait it out. It's not as if she could jump out of the car and make a run for it.

She'd deal with Michael when she saw him. She folded her arms and silently fumed, even as part of her bloomed with a macabre sense of excitement.

Forty minutes later, they took the exit to Sag Harbor. Mia jerked up on her seat and peered out the window.

The historic and quaint seaside town was elegantly quiet. The shops that were reminiscent of a postcard ad for weekend getaways were closed. The boats were docked and bobbing gently in the water.

The driver continued through the commercial section of town and drove to the outskirts, where the stately home of the wealthy African-American elite lived.

Finally, the driver turned into a cul-de-sac and pulled onto a gravel driveway.

Mia's door was pulled open and the driver extended his hand to help her out of the car. She stepped out and reflexively inhaled the heady scent of the sea and brisk night air. The sky had just begun to fill with stars and the half-moon seemed to hang perfectly above a two-story, sprawling white house that overlooked the ocean.

It was breathtaking.

"This way," the driver said, leading Mia up the path to the front door.

As she took the first of three steps, the door opened. Her gaze rose. Her heart leaped in her chest. She thought she was prepared to see him.

She wasn't.

Michael descended the stairs like a fantasy hero out of a dream.

Mia couldn't move, and before she could pull herself together, Michael was taking her hand and saying something to her, but she couldn't make out the words: they were being drowned out by the pounding of the pulse in her ears and the electricity that was surging through her from his touch.

"I'm glad you came."

Those four simple words stripped away the past, all the lost years and misgivings, and suddenly she was glad she'd come as well.

Michael could barely contain all that he was feeling inside. When he laid eyes on Mia, those words he spoke were no more than a smoke screen. He didn't want to make polite conversation. He wanted to take her and make her remember what it felt like to have him inside her, her body wound around his, her soft moans yielding to screams of release. That's what he wanted to do, but of course he couldn't. Instead, he apologized.

"Sorry for all the cloak-and-dagger," he began, guiding her

into a foyer the size of her entire condo. "But I knew if I told you where you were going, you would have refused."

"Still trying to make up my mind for me, I see."

That had always been a bone of contention between them. Michael wanted what Michael wanted, and he could never fathom why everyone didn't go along with him all the time.

He turned to face her and laughed lightly. "You're right. I should have given you the option. But now you're here." His chestnut-brown eyes meandered over her, taking in every inch.

He was still a gorgeous man to behold, Mia thought, an older, more mature version of Blair Underwood—a cool combination of boyish charm, dangerous sexuality and a ruthless streak that made for a lethal combination. The tinge of gray at his temples and the tiny flecks in his shadow of a beard only added to the dazzling package.

Michael was eight years her senior, but he was as fit as a man half his age. At forty-five, he had achieved what many only dreamed of and, knowing Michael, he'd only just begun.

Mia forced those thoughts to the back of her mind. He was a prime suspect in an illegal operation and she could not allow the intoxicating scent of his cologne, the glimmer in his eyes or the electricity of his touch to make her forget that.

"Please come in and sit down. I've had dinner prepared. But if you'd like that drink first—apple martini, right?" His smile lit up the room.

"You remembered."

"There isn't much about you that I've forgotten." His gaze held her.

Mia swallowed. "A drink will be fine, but I really can't stay for dinner."

Disappointment creased his eyes. But just as quickly the look was gone. He lightly ran his tongue across his lips and a shiver ran down Mia's spine.

"I see." His right brow flicked. "Then let's have that drink for old time's sake."

He walked ahead of her and stepped down into the sunken living room, which was something right out of *House Beautiful*. The shimmering teal-colored marble floors gave the illusion of walking on Caribbean water. Low contemporary furniture in a mix of fabrics and textures, all in cream and sandy-brown hues, dotted the space. Three-quarters of the room was wrapped in glass. The panoramic view looked out onto cliffs and oceans beyond. One wall encased a fireplace that would be perfect on a winter night, watching the powerful waves crash against the shore.

Mia set her purse on the glass coffee table while Michael fixed drinks. "You have a beautiful place."

Michael turned to her. "I had it built for you."

She couldn't have been more stunned if he'd slapped her. "For me?"

He offered a sad smile. "I'd always told you we'd have a place of our own one day." He lifted the bottle of vodka and poured some in a silver tumbler, followed by the apple martini mix and crushed ice. "I'm a man of my word." He capped the tumbler and shook it vigorously. "Got my divorce, too." His piercing look at her from over his shoulder held her in place.

Mia was speechless. A divorce. A house. It was everything she'd wanted. But it was too late. She was in love with Steven. And she couldn't let Michael's powers of persuasion or his unrelenting charm, this fabulous house or the fact that he was a free man dissuade her.

He crossed the room and handed her the drink.

"Thank you."

He raised his glass. "To old friends."

Cautiously, she touched her glass to his.

"I wanted to thank you for the referral," she said, needing to break the invisible hold he had on her.

He shrugged dismissively, walked a few paces and sat opposite her in the armchair that matched the couch, both covered in a butter-soft ecru-colored fabric that was so lush, the cushions so thick and soft, you could sink into it and never get up.

"I'm sure you didn't need the business. But I thought you'd be perfect for what they wanted."

"How would you know?"

He offered a slight smile. "As I said before, I've followed your career. I've even attended some of your events. Incognito, of course."

That confession shook her. "Why?"

He took a short swallow of his drink, studied the contents for a moment before speaking. "It was my way of staying in your life."

The answer was delivered so softly, so sincerely that it twisted her heart.

This couldn't be the man that Jean claimed might be behind an illegal escort service. This was the man she'd once loved. Standing before her was the man she'd prayed he would one day become. There was no way that the two could be one and the same.

"What are you thinking about?"

The gentle nudge of the words drew her back from her thoughts.

"Just that I never thought I'd see you again, especially like this, and that you've been following my career." She shifted her glass from her right hand to her left. "Which events did you attend?" she asked, the beginnings of a smile flickering around her mouth.

Michael chuckled. "The one on the yacht last year."

A flash of that event ran through her mind, along with the fact that the clients had turned out to be behind an identity theft ring that Danielle uncovered.

"How come I didn't see you? Why didn't you say anything?"

There was that shrug again. "I made sure that you didn't. I can blend in when I need to. Besides, there had to be at least three hundred people there and you were pretty busy."

"You could have said something."

"I thought it best not to. The last thing you wrote to me was not to contact you. So I figured the last thing you wanted was for me to show up at one of your events."

That bit of truth stung. She remembered the letter and the weeks that it took to compose it and finally mail it. She glanced away.

"How have you been, Mia?" he asked gently. "Without me. How have you been?"

What could she say? That she struggled to get him out of her system for nearly five years? That there were still times when she thought of him, remembered how they were together, the emptiness that she felt when she walked out of his life? Of course she couldn't say that.

"I've managed. My business keeps me busy."

All of a sudden, she looked up and he was standing over her. He took her glass from her hand and put it on the table, then took her hands and pulled her to her feet.

"I've missed you. Each and every day I've missed you. Everything that I do, dream or plan—you are in my thoughts. I want you back, Mia."

Her heart thundered. Her entire body was on fire. She could feel his energy wrap around her, draw her in, break down her will. And then his mouth was on hers and she couldn't move.

His mouth was warm, all-encompassing and incredibly sweet. She remembered those lips, the feel of them against her own. But when his tongue tentatively glided across her lips, then into the recesses of her mouth, she began to shake and he held her—held her firmly against him and she felt his longing, his need press hard and heavy between her thighs.

Her thoughts spun in a million directions at once, then crashed.

She pulled away, turned her head and stumbled back. "I can't do this." She shook her head.

He reached for her but she held up her hand to stop him. "Don't."

Michael stepped back. "I'm sorry. I shouldn't have done that."

She dared to look at him. All she saw was longing and sincerity in his expression.

Michael exhaled. "Can we start over?"

She sat down before she fell down and clasped her hands together atop her weak knees to keep them from shaking.

What she wanted to do was run as far as she could. But she couldn't do that and she couldn't alienate him. She needed to get inside his business, inside his life. But what was she willing to do to accomplish that?

Mia forced a tight smile. "Sure."

Michael seemed to sigh in relief. "Great. And to show you I really mean it, I'm gonna sit right here and not move a muscle until you're ready to go." He sat down on the lounger, folded his hands, pressed his knees together and plastered a contrite look on his face. The visual effect was hysterical and Mia burst out laughing.

Michael grinned. "That's how I like to see you, with that pretty smile on your face."

Mia smothered the rest of her giggles. "Can we talk about business now?"

Michael leaned back, then stretched out on the chaise longue. "Absolutely." He gave her the Reader's Digest version of Raven, the star he was hired to debut. She was nineteen for the public, but she was really twenty-two. Great voice, painfully shy, inked a major deal with Atlantic Records and her CD was scheduled to "drop" in two months. All the industry execs were to be invited, the cable stations, media and selected guests.

"Sounds simple enough. So why do I hear a *but* in there somewhere?"

"Our star doesn't want to do it."

"Oh… Why?"

"As I said, she's incredibly shy. She just wants to make music. So even though the studio wants a blowout event, we…you still need to make it feel intimate, so that our star doesn't freak out."

Mia nodded.

"Venue and setting are going to be crucial to make all parties concerned happy."

"Do you have a date in mind?"

"Three weeks."

Mia's eyes widened.

He shrugged. "My hands are tied on that one." He waited a beat. "You still want to do it?"

"Sure. I'll make it happen. No problem."

"Great. I'll have Brenda put all the information together for you and have it sent to your office."

She needed to get inside his office. "Hmm. I can pick it up. I'd like to see where you work."

He grinned. "Whenever you're ready."

"Tomorrow."

"A lady who doesn't waste time."

"As you said, no time like the present."

He put his feet on the floor and stood up. "Let me show you the rest of the house." He extended his hand to help her up.

"How long have you had this place?" she asked as he guided her with a hand at the small of her back to the kitchen.

"I was having it built when we were together. It was going to be my big surprise."

What! Her stomach did a somersault. He'd never said a word.

Michael turned on the light and the magnificent kitchen was suffused in soft track lighting. Racks of stainless-steel pots hung from the ceiling. And in sharp contrast to the modern feel of the living room, the kitchen was pure country. Glass-paneled French doors led to the back and would undoubtedly provide great lighting. Oak covered the floors and they gleamed. Freestanding hutches and corner cupboards provided plenty of storage space. A huge oak island sat in the center of the enormous kitchen and this is where the modern came in. Somehow, Michael had managed to have a wok, a grill and running water built into the island. A table for four was placed near the French doors and the open-faced cabinetry exhibited a chef's dream of condiments, pastas and spices. Another extraordinary touch was the restaurant-size refrigerator/freezer and built-in range. The meals she could fix in this space, she thought.

"I had you in mind when I had the kitchen done," he said softly, stepping up behind her.

She spun toward him, nearly colliding with him he was so close. She took a step back and drew in a sharp breath.

He angled his head to the side. "Maybe you'd like to come up one weekend and try out some of the stuff."

Mia swallowed over the knot in her throat. She turned away. "What about the rest of the house?" she said instead of responding to his offer.

"This way." He led her to the connecting room, which was the formal dining room. Then onto a small home theater that sat at least fifteen.

He opened another door. "I work in here whenever I come up for the weekend."

The room had two computers, shelves of books, a fax, a phone and what appeared to be a scanner.

"How often is that?"

He closed the door. "At least twice a month."

She made a mental note. "I see you still keep your computers on even when you're not using them."

"Old habits, I guess. Back here are the two guest rooms, and baths." He flung open two doors that were side by side. "This is the master bedroom." He opened the door.

It was totally Michael. Rich, lush, completely masculine with bold browns and bronzes, a king-size bed and a television that was almost as big. She glanced across the room and was stunned to see a framed photograph of the two of them on the dresser.

She remembered the day they'd taken it. It was the week before Christmas and the first snow had fallen. Michael had gotten tickets to see *The Nutcracker* at Radio City Music Hall. When they came out, a photographer who was hawking his wares offered to take their picture. She was staring up into his eyes with a bold smile and his look showed total adoration.

"We were happy," he said gently.

She flinched. It was as if he'd read her mind. "Michael…"

"I know, I know…I'm sorry." He held up his hands in supplication.

"I probably should be going."

He nodded. "I'll get Carl to bring the car around."

They went back up front. She needed just a few minutes alone. She picked up her purse. "Uh, I'm going to use the restroom."

"Sure. Straight back, left then right."

She left him in the living room and found his office. Listening for any footsteps, she quickly went inside, opened her purse and took out a CD. She silently prayed that he was actually logged on so that she wouldn't be stymied by a password.

She hit the Enter key and the desktop opened. She released a sigh of relief, put in the CD and listened to it whirr while it planted a tracking program onto the hard drive. The CD popped out. She tucked it in her purse, hurried out then headed back up front.

Michael looked up when she entered the room. "Carl is out front. He'll take you home." He walked her to the door.

At the door he asked, "Are you sure you want to work on this project? We'll have to see a lot of each other."

She looked directly at him. "I'm a big girl, Michael. And this is business. Right?"

He leaned down and gently kissed her cheek. "Get home safely, Mia," he said, avoiding her question.

She looked at him for a moment before turning away and walking toward the waiting car.

It's business. I love Steven. It's business. I love Steven. She repeated that mantra all the way back to the city.

Chapter 6

By the time Mia turned the key in the lock of her front door, it was nearly eleven. She'd wracked her brains trying to come up with some plausible explanation as to where she could have been until now. Nothing sounded remotely legitimate.

When she stepped in, she fully expected Steven to be sitting on the couch waiting for her. He wasn't.

She walked through the front of the condo to the bedroom in the back. Even in the moonlight she could tell that the room was empty. She switched on the light and looked around.

The bed was still made. Absently, she put her purse down on top of the dresser and walked to the bathroom. Empty. Where was Steven?

She made an about-face, returned to the front of the apartment and went into the kitchen. That's when she saw the note on the fridge.

She snatched it down and read it.

Hey, babe, decided at the last minute to have a boys' night out. Hanging with Blake, Nick and Bernard. We're celebrating one of the guys on the job's birthday. Tried your cell. Went straight to voice mail. Don't wait up. Luv ya.

She didn't know whether to be relieved or pissed off. She took the note and tossed it in the trash. On the one hand, she didn't have to explain her own late night. On the other, if she'd known that Steven would be late, she might have stayed longer. What did that mean?

She frowned, thinking of the note again...*went straight to voice mail.* Ohhh, of course. She'd turned her phone off in the event that Steven did call while she was with Michael. That way she wouldn't have been caught in the uncomfortable position of talking to her current lover while her ex-lover listened to every word.

Well, at least this time she was off the explanation hook. This time.

Mia retrieved her cell phone from her purse on the hall table and turned it back on. Sure enough, there were three missed calls. She dialed into her voice-mail service and listened.

The first message was from Steven, pretty much saying what the note did. The second call was from Danielle, checking in with her, and the third was from Ashley.

"I hope everything went okay. If you want to talk tomorrow, I'm here."

She hit the delete code and pressed the phone to her chest.

Did it go okay? The minute she saw Michael, she'd lost control of her senses. She'd let him kiss her and she'd kissed him back. And what about her feelings when she realized that Steven wasn't home and that if she had known he was going to be late she would have stayed longer?

Mia walked into the bedroom. Did all that equal *okay?* She caught a glimpse of herself in the oval mirror above the dresser. If she didn't know better, she'd swear she could see

Scarlet Woman plastered across her forehead. At the very least *Guilty*.

She stepped out of her shoes and put them in the rack in the closet.

She'd betrayed Steven. She'd betrayed their relationship. She massaged her temples. How could she have been so weak?

The sensation of that kiss snuck up on her and a sudden heat suffused her body.

Vigorously she shook her head. It was the first and the last time, she vowed. She had a job to do. Michael Burke was an assignment, and that was it. She was in love with Steven. And she could not allow herself to forget that ever again. No matter what.

With that determination at the forefront of her mind, she went to the closet, took out the shoe boxes and opened the panel where she kept her kit. Quickly she removed it.

Meticulously inventorying the contents, she removed the eye-shadow case, the pressed powder compact and a tube of mascara. She would need all these items when she met Michael at his office. The eye shadow concealed a mini-recording disk that could stick to any surface. The compact doubled as a camera, and the mascara was actually a memory stick that she would use to download files from his computer—if the opportunity presented itself. She put all these items in her tote bag.

Before Steven came home, she wanted to sync her PDA with Michael's computer. Although he didn't go to the Sag Harbor house often, he did mention that he used that computer for work. It was worth a shot.

Mia turned on her PDA and scrolled to the *Find Me* program that would allow her to look inside Michael's computer, see his files and actually open them remotely. She keyed in the access code and after several moments the screen read that she was connected.

Her heart thumped in concert with the opening of the front door. Her head jerked up from the information in front of her. "Mia!"

She took a quick look around to be sure she hadn't left anything out, then turned the PDA off and dropped it in her tote. She darted into the bathroom and turned on the shower.

"Hey, babe," he called out over the rush of water. "Sorry I'm so late."

Mia peeled off her clothes, tossed them in a pile on the floor and ducked into the shower.

The bathroom door inched open and Steven stuck his head in. "Hey, sweetie, mind some company?"

Mia pulled the shower curtain partially back and smiled in greeting. "Love some."

Later that night, as Mia lay curled in Steven's embrace and their racing hearts had settled, she thought with alarm that it was the very first time that Steven had not satisfied her.

Chapter 7

Mia was totally distracted at work the following day and as hard as she tried she couldn't concentrate on the monthly financial report. The numbers seemed to jump all over the page just to torment her.

Frustrated, she pushed the pages aside and stared blankly at the screen saver on her computer. She glanced up at the clock above her office door.

Still two hours before she was due to be at Michael's office. Maybe she'd get lucky and not have to see him. But that, of course, would defeat the whole purpose of her going. She needed access to his office, his phone and his computer.

But what troubled her most was what had happened—or had not happened—last night between her and Steven. Not to mention this morning. She and Steven always had sex in the morning, and at the very least a stimulating touching and kissing session as they prepared for their day, leading to heightened anticipation at night.

But this morning she wasn't in her usual playful, teasing mood, and although Steven had given her several long, lingering kisses, he didn't pursue anything further.

Had he realized that she hadn't climaxed last night? Did it bother him? Did he care? And then an awful thought leaped into her mind. Was he seeing someone else?

The sharp knock on her door jerked some sense into her. It was her own guilty conscience, she knew, that had her conjuring up dalliances about Steven. She shook her head.

"Come in."

Ashley stepped through the doorway. "I worked out a preliminary plan for the boutique. If you want to take a look at it, I put it in New Projects on the shared drive."

"Thanks." She forced a smile but couldn't look Ashley in the eye. She'd done everything short of taking in dirty laundry from a stranger to keep herself busy so that Ashley wouldn't ask her about last night. For the better part of the morning, she'd been able to avoid her. Until now.

"I'll, um, look at it, but I'm sure it's fine." She studied the first line of a memo she held in front of her as if it could block out reality and what she was certain was Ashley's inquiring gaze.

"Look, I want you to know that it's okay to talk to me and it's okay to look at me. If you don't want to discuss last night or our conversation yesterday—ever—it's fine. Seriously." She took a step closer. "I won't judge you. I thought I was your friend. And I value the confidence you put in me." She drew in a breath and stood straighter. "That's my spiel for today."

"I'm meeting him at his office today," she blurted out and looked up at Ashley with something akin to fear in her eyes.

"Why?" she softly asked.

Mia curled her fingers into fists on her desk. "I have to." She struggled with the words, the burning in her stomach.

Ashley frowned in confusion. "You. Mia Turner never *had* to do anything, especially something that she is obviously having an issue with." She tentatively sat down, reached across the desk and put all the phone lines on hold. She turned to Mia. "If you want to talk, I'm listening. And there is no one to disturb us." She waited.

Dozens of thoughts raced through Mia's mind. *Last night, seeing Michael again, the kiss, the sex with Steven, her guilt, her assignment, the Cartel, her oath.* They all ran together until her head began to pound and panic seized her. Her life and emotions were suddenly out of control and she didn't know how to handle it.

Finally, she released her clenched fists, raised her gaze and focused on Ashley. There were obviously things she could not disclose, which would make her having to see Michael difficult to explain. She cleared her throat.

"I'm going to tell you some things. Some are not going to make any sense because of the things that I *can't* tell you. Understand?"

Ashley blinked in confusion. "Not really, but go ahead. I'll piece it together."

"Well, you already know about me and Michael's past…"

Ashley nodded.

"Last night he didn't take me for drinks. He had his driver take me to his home on Sag Harbor, the home he said he'd had built for me and him."

Ashley sucked in a breath of surprise, but didn't interrupt.

Mia swallowed. "He kissed me. And I didn't stop him."

From there the rest of the story poured out: how she felt, her confusion, even what happened between her and Steven, her guilt.

She rubbed her forehead as if the action could rub away the thoughts and images that tramped through her brain.

"Wow," Ashley murmured after Mia had finished. "And I guess the reason why you have to go see him is the part you can't tell me."

Mia nodded.

"Why not let me go with you?"

"I wish I could but I can't. All I can say is that it's bigger than me and you and I promised that I would do this."

Ashley blew out a breath. "I respect that. But can I offer some advice?"

"I could use some."

"Be clear about the why. Be sure that you're doing this because you have no choice and not because you subconsciously want to rekindle your relationship. Because if you do, you owe it to Steven to be honest with him about your feelings."

How could she explain that it was a combination of both? A part of her felt duty-bound and another part wanted to see what life would be like again with Michael. In addition to which, she wanted to prove that he couldn't be capable of the things he was suspected of. And she hoped that her own misgivings would not cloud her judgment.

Ashley pushed up from her seat. "If you change your mind, I'm free all afternoon," she said with a soft smile. She turned to leave.

"Wait!"

Ashley turned back around.

Mia stood. "If I take you with me, you have to promise not to ask any questions, no matter what happens."

"Gee, Mia, you sound like some kind of spy or something."

Mia snatched up her purse and tote bag. She looked Ashley in her eyes. "Or something." She headed for the door, leaving Ashley pinned in place by her declaration. "Coming?"

Ashley hurried behind her boss and wondered what she'd gotten herself into.

Chapter 8

"No point in circling the block again," Mia groused, look-ing above and below car tops and along the tightly packed street as she inched down 56th Street. Michael's office on Madison Avenue was in the heart of Manhattan. But parking on Madison was out of the question. "It's mostly either No Parking Anytime or For Commercial Traffic Only."

"There's a garage about a block down on your right." Ashley pointed out.

Mia signaled then eased into the right lane in front of a yellow cab and zipped across the intersection before the light changed. The Quick-Park parking garage was franchised throughout the city. Their trademark black and gold signs were like beacons of salvation for harried drivers.

Throughout the thirty-minute drive, Ashley had refrained from asking questions, basically making small talk or keeping quiet, which totally went against her grain. This entire sce-nario had Ashley deeply concerned about Mia. Mia had said there were things she couldn't tell her, and heaven only knew what that meant. She just hoped that whatever Mia had gotten herself involved in was not going to get her hurt, and she didn't mean physically.

During the months that she'd spent working with Mia, she'd come to admire and respect her. Mia was forthright, professional, loyal to her friends and able to charm the most difficult clients. She ran her business with precision, and she conducted her life with the same kind of order and attention to detail—all without breaking a sweat. Which was why it was so unsettling to see her like this—totally distracted, edgy and, for lack of a better word, scared. Those were words Ashley would have never associated with Mia, and Ashley vowed to stick by her side and see things through.

Mia unsnapped her seat belt, pulled down the overhead mirror and reapplied her lipstick, which she'd pretty much chewed off during the trip.

For an instant she froze. The look in her eyes that was reflected back at her was one of uncertainty and confusion. And she knew that it had more to do with her twisted feelings for Michael than her ability to do her job. Yet both were intricately intertwined, and she couldn't see one without the other. But she had to.

She felt Ashley staring at her and turned. "I may need your help."

Ashley's honey-brown eyes widened ever so slightly. "Sure. Whatever you need."

Mia offered a tight-lipped smile, flipped the mirror back in place, grabbed her purse and tote and hopped out.

The attendant handed her a ticket and asked how long she would be.

"No more than an hour." She turned and walked up the ramp and out onto the busy street.

Michael's offices were on the five-hundred block of Madison Avenue, surrounded by the headquarters of all the major banks both domestic and foreign and the leading financial institutions, Schwaab, Deutschebank. His office was at 554-11 Madison on the twenty-second floor.

The duo pushed through the glass-and-chrome revolving doors. They were stopped at the security check-in desk, and asked to produce identification and sign a logbook.

Ever since 9/11, all the major New York City office buildings had instituted this procedure. Mia often wondered what possible good it would do and what kind of deterrent it was for someone who really wanted to do harm. There was no way to prove that anyone's ID was legitimate.

Her friend Danielle's last Cartel case was a perfect example of what people could do with ID. Dani's identity theft case even added an additional element of finding famous look-alikes who were used to gain access to parties, offices and homes with the purpose of stealing unsuspecting victims' identities. The successful outcome was all in the news, with no mention of Danielle or the Cartel, of course.

No matter how careful you were and no matter how many safeguards were put in place, someone, somewhere, was working to breach your defenses. The Ladies Cartel was a testament to that truth. Besides, she reasoned, if someone intended to get in and blow up a building, the logbook would be destroyed in the process. It was all quite arcane and silly in Mia's mind, but if it offered some sense of security, she supposed it was useful.

Mia and Ashley walked side by side to the second bank of elevators after signing in.

Mia watched the dial of the elevator as the lights did a countdown. "I may need you to keep his executive assistant—and possibly Michael—busy," she said without looking at Ashley.

"Sure. No problem. Busy I can do."

The elevator doors slid open and deposited a half dozen people into the lobby. Mia and Ashley were the only two to get on.

"If I say I want to use the restroom, I'm going to need you to keep everyone occupied. At least for five minutes. If we get to sit in Michael's office, I'm going to need you to get him out of it."

"How?"

"We'll think of something."

The bell dinged and the doors slid open.

"This would be so much more fun if you told me what you couldn't tell me," Ashley said under her breath.

Mia tossed her a look and stepped off the elevator. The directional signs indicated that the Avante Enterprises offices were to the right. They turned toward a set of glass doors.

A receptionist looked up at their approach. "May I help you?" Her perky voice came through the intercom embedded in the wall. Mia recognized it from the phone call. She stepped closer to the intercom.

"Mia Turner. I have an appointment with Mr. Burke."

The door buzzed, along with the sound of the lock disengaging. Mia grabbed the large chrome handle and pushed the door open.

"If you will have a seat, I'll let Mr. Burke know you're here."

"Thank you," Mia murmured and took a seat with Ashley right next to her.

"Nice digs," Ashley said.

"Hmm." Interesting, she thought, as she took in the décor of the reception area. The colors were in sharp contrast to the house on the harbor. Here black dominated, with gray and burgundy accents. The colors and coordinating décor spoke power, style and control. All nouns easily associated with Michael Burke.

Moments later, a woman of about thirty with a cap of silky black curls outlining a perfectly made-up face approached them. Mia instinctively knew this was Ms. Executive Assistant.

The woman's chocolate chip–pinstriped suit jacket hugged her narrow waist, fanned out ever so slightly to caress her hips, and the above-the-knee-length skirt showcased the legs of a dancer—long, lean, perfectly formed and strong. She seemed to instinctively know one from the other and extended her hand to Mia.

"Ms. Turner. I'm Brenda Forde. I believe we've met via phone." She directed intense honey-colored eyes at Mia, all the more disconcerting because of their lightness against her flawlessly brown skin and the fierceness that hovered in them.

Real or contacts, Mia wondered in a comedic moment.

"Yes. We have met, haven't we? Always good to put a face with a voice." She released the butter-soft hand and turned to Ashley. "This is *my* executive assistant and business manager, Ashley Temple."

Ashley extended her hand. "Nice to meet you."

Brenda gave a short nod of her head. "If you'll follow me, I'll get you settled in the small conference room. Michael…Mr. Burke is on a business call. As soon as he's done, he'll join us."

There goes that *us* again, Mia thought. She smiled and followed Brenda down the short hallway and was led to a room with, unfortunately, a glass door and walls.

"Please make yourselves comfortable. Would you like something to drink while you wait?"

"Some water for me," Mia said.

"Water is fine," Ashley added.

"I'll be right back." She picked up a remote from the table and pointed it at a television mounted onto the wall. The CNN studio filled the screen. "Michael likes CNN," Brenda said with a smile that held a challenge.

"I remember," Mia tossed back, unable to help herself and secretly delighted in seeing Ms. Executive Assistant flinch before she walked out.

"Meow, meow," Ashley sang. "At least let me know when to duck out of the way of the claws. What was that about?"

Mia quickly gave her the rundown of her earlier conversation with Brenda.

"You think they're seeing each other?"

Mia gave a slight shrug. "If not, she certainly wants to. Not that it's any of my business," she added quickly.

Ashley bit back a smile.

Mia reluctantly pulled her glasses out of her purse. She took a good look around the room. The conference table took up most of the space, surrounded by eleven chairs, five on each side and one at the head. Two computer stations braced one wall. With her growing knowledge of electronics and technology, she noted that there were microphones built into the table, which let her know that conversations here were recorded. The wall panel that controlled the television also controlled the screen that could be lowered from the ceiling. She was pretty sure it included teleconferencing, which would account for the video camera in the back of the room.

Her instincts told her this room was used for meetings much more sensitive than who would be the next R & B star, which gave her even more reason to want to tap it. What solidified her resolve was the camera that she'd spotted hidden between the panels on the wall. It was no bigger than a quarter and to those who were none the wiser it looked like an imperfection in the wall. A hidden camera would certainly limit what she could get away with in this room. The ideal situation would be to find Avante's control room.

Mia glanced toward the door. Brenda and Michael were coming in. Mia couldn't miss the adoring look that Brenda gave Michael as he held the door open for her. Mia took off her glasses and returned them to her purse.

Ashley stole a look in Mia's direction as the doors swung open.

"Mia." Michael came right to her, braced her shoulders and kissed her cheek. "Had to bring backup, huh," he teased, whispering in her ear. He stepped back and looked her in the eye, as if she was the only person in the room.

Mia swallowed over the tightness in her throat. The intoxicating scent of him momentarily clouded her thoughts. "Michael, my executive assistant, Ashley Temple."

"My pleasure, Ms. Temple," he said, finally focusing on something other than Mia. He shook Ashley's hand, then turned back to Mia. "Would you prefer to talk here or over lunch?"

"Here is fine. Ashley has prepared a PowerPoint presentation for our proposal. Then we can have lunch. If that works for you." She smiled sweetly.

"Not a problem."

Ashley took the printed copies out of the leather folder she carried, along with the CD of the presentation. She handed out the literature.

Mia's heart pounded. She hoped that Michael would allow them to use the computer to run the program and not just the projector.

"All this technology is not my thing," Michael admitted. "That's Brenda's area of expertise." He tossed his hands up in the air in a gesture of exasperation.

"Is your computer linked to the video screen?" Mia asked.

"Of course. I'll get you set up." Brenda went to one of the computers and turned it on. She lowered the lights then depressed a button on the wall panel and the screen descended. "You can load your CD."

Ashley went to the computer and inserted the CD.

Mia's heart was pounding. If there was one glitch in the program that she'd embedded on the CD, they were toast. After Ashley had completed the PowerPoint proposal, Mia had volunteered to put it on the CD. Later that evening, Mia wrote a code—with the help of Jasmine at Cartel headquarters—that would track the activities of the computer and was activated when the PowerPoint was shown.

What it gave Mia the opportunity to do was look inside the computer files in addition to mirroring every keystroke.

The screen filled with MT Management's logo and its tagline, "Your dream event is our reality."

For about ten seconds the screen froze then flickered. Mia held her breath. Jasmine had warned her about this and advised her not to panic. She'd been meticulous about entering the code. She'd gone over it three times to be sure she'd typed in the correct HTML string.

The first screen finally opened and Mia exhaled as Ashley's voice gave the text and images verbal support.

While everyone was engrossed in the presentation, Mia felt around inside her tote bag, which she held on her lap beneath the table, and unzipped her "go bag"—her little carryall that held some of her tools of the trade. It looked like a makeup pouch. She felt around for the recording disk that looked like an eye-shadow pot. She had to unscrew the cap and lift the disk out. It was no bigger than a dime and nearly slipped from her fingers. One side was sticky and would adhere to any surface, virtually inconspicuous. She pressed the sticky side underneath the table, felt it to be sure it was secure then dropped the circular pot back into her go bag.

Ashley had about three more minutes. Mia began to breathe a little easier.

"I'm impressed," Michael said when the screen went blank.

Brenda turned on the lights.

"How soon can you get started?"

"Michael—" Brenda cut in.

He held up his hand.

Mia and Ashley glanced at each other.

"As soon as you're ready," Mia answered.

"That's what I like to hear." He stood. "Let's seal the deal over lunch."

Mia tossed a triumphant grin in Brenda's direction. Triumphant in more ways than one.

As they walked out, Mia hesitated. "I need to use the restroom."

"I'll take you," Brenda offered.

"That's fine. Just tell me where it is. I'm sure I can find it myself."

"I'd love to see the rest of your space," Ashley chimed in, hearing her cue.

"Sure," Michael agreed. "Mia, we'll meet you up front."

"Down the hall, make two lefts," Brenda reluctantly instructed Mia.

"Thanks. I won't be a minute." She walked in the general direction of the restroom. She decided it would be pointless to try to get in the control room, but Michael's office was a different story.

She hurried down the hall, passing a few employees along the way, who didn't pay much attention to her. She glanced at the nameplates on the doors. The offices were set up like a maze: short hallways that led to different departments, quick turns and dead ends. She felt as if she should have left bread crumbs so she could find her way back.

Finally, she found Michael's office after following a sign for administration. She hoped that it wasn't locked. She tried the knob and the door opened. Taking a quick look left then right, she stepped inside and shut the door behind her.

Mia was pretty certain that if Michael were involved in anything, the last place he would have microphones and cameras would be in his office.

The rectangular office screamed masculine. Brown leather furnishings, vertical floor-to-ceiling blinds in a bronze color that gave the room a warm glow. An antique oval rug covered the center of the wood floor. His desk was pure Michael—rich and dark. His mantra screen saver crawled across the monitor: *"I'm dreaming of great things and doing them."*

She went directly to his desk. The first thing she did was insert a recording device into his phone, then she took a CD out of her bag and put it in the computer. After it loaded, she hit the Enter key and the disk whirred then exited.

Mia checked her watch. She'd been gone a little more than five minutes. Hopefully, Ashley was running her mouth and asking a zillion questions. She took one last look around, went to the door and cracked it open. The hallway was empty. She stepped out and shut the door behind her.

Briskly she walked down the hallway, turned right and ran smack into Brenda.

"Oh, I'm so sorry," Mia sputtered. She pressed her hand to her chest.

Brenda stared at her. "This isn't the way to the ladies' room."

Mia smiled and shook her head. "I got totally turned around. I should have taken you up on your offer."

"It's this way," she said with quiet deliberation. She extended her hand in the opposite direction.

Mia clutched her purse tighter in her hand and secured her tote on her shoulder. "Thanks." She followed Brenda to the door with the image of a woman emblazoned on the front. Mia pushed the door open.

"I'll wait for you so you don't get lost again."

"'Preciate that." Mia stepped inside and nearly collapsed

against the door. Another minute and Brenda would have seen her coming out of Michael's office.

She walked to the sink, turned on the cold water and looked at her reflection. "This is only the beginning," she said to the reflection, "so get it together."

Mia ran her wrists under the cold tap water to slow down her racing heart and lower the heat in her body that was making her light-headed. She dried her hands then took her lipstick from her purse and touched up her mouth.

Brenda was leaning against the wall when Mia stepped out.

"All done!" she said with a cheery smile.

Brenda stepped up to her, so close that Mia noticed she was wearing individual false eyelashes and a couple of them had come out.

"I don't know what your deal is," Brenda said with chilly calm. "But stay away from Michael." With that she spun away on her two-inch heels before Mia could digest the veiled threat and deliver a comeback.

Stirred but not shaken, Mia followed the scent of Brenda's perfume and joined the trio at the receptionist's desk.

Brenda Forde was going to be a problem.

Chapter 9

"You've been pretty quiet today," Blake Fields said to Steven as they reviewed the blueprints for a co-op they were helping to develop. "Everything cool?"

In Steven's circle of friends, Blake was at the center. They'd been tight since college. Steven was Blake's best man when he married Savannah and was godfather to their daughter Mikayla. They'd shared a great deal through the years, the good and the bad, and they never lied to each other, no matter how much the truth might sting. That was the cornerstone of their friendship. If there was anyone that he could talk to about what may be going on with Mia, it was Blake. It helped, too, that Blake's wife was Mia's best friend.

Steven put down his drafting pencil and looked across the table to Blake, who was rerolling the blueprints that needed to be stored.

Blake turned from the pigeonhole where the blueprints

were kept and focused on Steven. His brows drew together in concern. "I'm listening."

Steven linked his fingers together while his tumbling thoughts settled down. "It's about Mia."

The frown line deepened. "Is she okay? She's not ill…pregnant?"

Steven released a short chuckled. "Naw, none of the above."

"Oh, cool. So what is it?"

"Man, I don't even know where to start or if I'm making something out of nothing."

"Start at the spot that's buggin' you the most."

He ran his tongue across his lips and blew out a breath, leaning slightly forward. "Me and Mia have this bangin' sex life, no pun intended. Anyway, lately she hasn't been there, ya know what I mean?"

Blake nodded.

"I know my woman. I know her body and I know when she's faking."

Blake's eyes widened.

"She acts like she's into it but I can tell she's not. And last night…" His voice drifted off. He wasn't sure that he was ready to tell his buddy that he couldn't satisfy his woman.

"Have you talked to her?"

"I'd feel like an idiot. It's probably just in my head."

"If it's in your head, it got there for a reason."

Steven was silent for a moment, trying to pinpoint the date and source of his unease. "I guess it started about two weeks ago. She's been distracted and kinda secretive. I mean, I've walked in on her a couple of times and she shuts the computer off or abruptly ends a call. And she's been evasive when I ask what she was working on. Then the whole sex thing." He looked away.

Blake was quiet for a moment. He'd been in Steven's

shoes, or at least his wife, Savannah, had been in Steven's shoes. Tristan Montgomery—a client—had decided that she wanted Blake as an addendum to their business contract, and she made life very difficult for him, to a point that he seriously considered ending the contract, returning the money and moving on. The tension played havoc with his marriage and Tristan's tireless come-ons could wear down the best of men. But he couldn't imagine that someone was hovering in the background of Steven and Mia's relationship. Unfortunately, however, anything was possible even in the best relationship.

"Look, man," Blake said, straddling a chair and bracing his forearms along the top. "You know the mess I went through with Tristan. The only thing that saved me and Savannah was talking. Once I let Savannah know what was really going on, it removed her doubts, it gave me strength and then as a team we dealt with it together."

"I guess the thing that shakes me the most is that it's always been me who was holding all the cards, the one who raised the questions, the one who got to walk away."

"Hey, hold on. That's taking it to the extreme, don't you think?"

"I know, I know, I'm just saying…I feel out of my element. I've never let a woman get this close to me. And move in with a woman!" He snorted. "I took a big chance with Mia. If she messes over me…" He shook his head.

"We all thought we were playas until the right woman came along. Even you couldn't outplay me until Savannah came along," he teased.

That drew an appreciative chuckle from Steven. "So whatcha sayin'? I'm your wingman?"

"And a damn good one, too," Blake said, laughter rumbling over his words. "Bottom line, my brother, you have to admit that your playa card had been pulled. And the sooner you accept that and give in to what you feel for her, all that other macho BS about being in control and in charge won't mean jack. But you gotta talk to her. Tell her how you feel, what's been on your mind."

The waning afternoon light played on Steven's eyes, turning them a darker shade of grayish green.

"Yeah, guess I'm gonna have to. This just isn't my thing, spilling my guts."

Blake gave a crooked smile. "You'll get used to it."

"Do me a favor."

"Sure."

"See if you can pick Savannah's brain. Maybe Mia might have said something to her."

"I'll try. But haven't you heard of the girlfriend oath?"

Steven frowned. "The girlfriend oath?"

"Yeah, no boys allowed."

When Steven arrived home, he had every intention of talking with Mia, as Blake had suggested. But the truth was, talking about insecurities and being vulnerable to a woman didn't sit well with him.

He lived by the example set by his father. A man was a man. Men didn't cry, show fear or give in to their emotions. You never let a woman get beyond those defenses, no matter how much you loved them. If a woman could get to you in that way, then your enemies could get to you through her.

His father, Frank Long, had been a street hustler since his early teens and carried the mantra of the street deep in his soul. Although Steven knew that his father loved his mother, there were never open displays of affection or words of love tossed freely around. Frank showed his love through things. They had a stunning home on Sugar Hill in Harlem. His mother had more jewelry than she would ever wear, and he and his brother and sister never wanted for anything.

It was his mother, Grace, who provided the affection, some softness in their lives, but his father's lessons and the way he lived his life were heavily ingrained in Steven.

He knew he felt deeply for Mia, more than any woman he'd been with. She anchored him and he didn't want to be with anyone else—this was a first for him. Having more than one woman at a time had been a way of life for him. It kept him from becoming too involved, caring too much. Steven Long was a playa to his heart, but as Blake had clearly pointed out, Mia had pulled his card.

Did that mean he was in love? Or in deep like? It must be something, he thought as he tugged off his tie en route to the bedroom. He'd given up his bachelor pad and moved in with Mia. That had to mean something, which made how Mia had been acting all the more unnerving for him.

He flicked on the bedroom light, took off his jacket and tossed it on the lounge chair near the window. He pulled the curtain back and gazed out at the street below.

Twilight was settling over the city. That in-between time of day and night when your eyes played tricks on you and things weren't quite as they seemed.

Just as he was about to turn away, he saw Mia's Lexus pull up in front of the building. He waited for her to exit. He loved to see her walk. When she didn't get out, he grew curious. He peered a bit closer and the outline of her body was defined by the streetlights. She had her head down on the steering wheel. And several times she hit the wheel with her palm.

Finally, she sat up, flipped down the mirror and checked her appearance. Then sat for a couple of minutes more before she gathered her things and got out. He watched her approach the building; the usual bounce and sway in her step was missing. Mia usually walked as if she was ready to take over the world—head held high, long smooth strides, determination etched on her face. But tonight her body language shouted defeat.

He turned away from the window once he saw her enter the building. Something must have happened at the office or with a client or with one of her friends. Mia never got rattled, so it had to be something major. Whatever it was, they'd deal with it. He heard her key in the door and went up front to meet her.

She came in and when she glanced up and saw him standing there, a smile to light up Broadway bloomed across her mouth.

"Hey," she greeted him. She pranced over to him and kissed him softly and briefly on the lips. "How was your day?"

"Fine," he murmured, totally confused by the woman he'd seen outside only moments ago who was obviously upset and the woman standing in front of him who acted as if the world was hers for the taking.

She brushed his cheek with her fingertip and moved past him. "Hungry?" she called out over her shoulder.

"No. I'm good. Late lunch." He followed her into the bedroom. "So how was your day? Anything exciting happen?"

"Not really." She gave him the benefit of a quick look before sitting on the side of the bed to take off her shoes.

Whatever was on her mind, she apparently didn't want to share it with him. He turned abruptly and headed back to the bedroom.

Moments later Mia heard the sound of the evening news coming from the living-room television.

Briefly she let down her guard and the weight of her day consumed her. The tension she dealt with at Michael's office while she planted the devices, followed by a two-hour lunch with him, Brenda and Ashley, all came closing in on her at once. They'd been seated in a booth for four and Michael took the liberty of sitting next to Mia.

Although lunch was very businesslike and aboveboard, she couldn't mistake the intermittent bump of thighs beneath the table or the brush of fingertips as they reached for the same item.

She could barely concentrate on the conversation going on around her and then as they left Michael was right behind her and whispered, "I want to make love to you, and I will."

The words were as much a promise as a threat. Michael Burke never said he would do anything without fully intending to do it.

When she and Ashley returned to their office, Mia was unusually subdued, but that didn't stop Ashley from voicing her opinion.

"I can see why you and a hundred other women would be attracted to Michael Burke," she said, taking a seat opposite Mia's desk without being asked. "And I also see that he still cares about you. But the only thing that really concerns me is that I see the same thing in you for him."

Mia's eyes flashed in Ashley's direction. She started to debate the point, but it was useless. She did have feelings for Michael. What they were she wasn't sure, but they were there just beneath the surface. She covered her face then finally found the courage to look at Ashley.

"I don't know what to do," she finally said.

"Look, I can take over this account so you won't have to deal with him."

"If I could have you do that, I would in a heartbeat."

"This is the part you can't talk about." It was more of a statement than a question.

Mia nodded.

"Then I'm fresh out of suggestions." She pushed up from the seat. "But whatever I can do to help, let me know."

"Thanks."

* * *

"Is something bothering you?"

Mia's head snapped up. She turned toward the doorway. Steven was standing there.

"Just a little tired, I guess. Kinda busy day at work. Nothing that a hot bath and a good night's sleep won't cure."

"You sure that's it?"

"Yes. Why?"

He rocked his jaw a minute. He started to tell her that he'd seen her in the car and had been standing in the doorway while she sat motionless and totally unaware of him. But he didn't want to hear her lie to him anymore.

"Nothing. Just asking. Look, I'm going to run out for a while."

"Oh." Mia focused on him as if seeing him for the first time. "Out?"

"Yes. Out. I'll see you later." Without further explanation he turned and walked away.

Mia sat there for a moment, too drained to react. It was probably best that Steven did go out for a while, she reasoned. She needed some time to push away Michael's words, wash away the heat of his breath on the back of her neck, the touch of his hand at the small of her back and the look in his eyes that said, *I'm coming for you.*

Her cell phone chirped. She dug it out of her tote and immediately recognized the number.

"Hello, Jean."

"I'm calling to remind you that I'm going to need an update from you by the end of the week."

"Of course."

"How much progress have you made?"

"I've made contact and I've established an opportunity to get inside the company."

"Excellent. I knew you would be the perfect one for this

assignment. I'll expect a complete update." She clicked off without so much as a goodbye.

However, as much as Mia didn't want to admit it, Jean's call was just the kick start that she needed. With Steven out of the house, it was the perfect time to check and sync all the devices. If she got really lucky, she might hear something worthwhile.

Chapter 10

Steven got in his BMW and headed off with no particular destination in mind. Driving usually cleared his head, especially when he was working on a difficult design problem. He usually didn't take evening drives to get his head right regarding relationships. If he drove somewhere, it was either home or away for good.

This was different. But everything about his and Mia's relationship was different. He was treading in brand-new territory and he had no idea where the land mines were.

He took the exit to the West Side Highway and headed south toward the Chelsea Piers.

The area had been totally revitalized over the past few years with bike and roller-skating lanes, benches and trees. The set for *Law & Order* was inside the pier as well, just off 23rd Street.

He slowed, pulled into one of the parking areas and got out. If there was one thing that could always be counted on in New York, it was that there was guaranteed to be people out doing something no matter the time, day or the weather. Truly, the city that never sleeps.

Steven set the alarm on his car and began to stroll along the docks. Anchored crafts bobbed in the water and the masts of the massive, once-military vessels, jutted toward the darkened skies.

A young couple Rollerblading streaked past him, followed by several joggers. A stiff fall breeze blew in from the water. He drew up the collar of his jacket around his neck. Lights ahead drew his attention and he walked toward them.

On one of the commercial strips was a small restaurant and bar located next to a bowling alley that was also still open for business. He decided to go into the restaurant.

"Good evening," said a young woman dressed in black. "Will you be having dinner or would you prefer to sit at the bar?"

"The bar is fine. Thanks."

"Up the stairs to the left. Enjoy your evening."

Steven walked toward the bar and found an empty seat in the middle of the horseshoe-shaped counter.

"What can I get for you this evening?"

Steven glanced up.

"Steven? Steven Long?"

He focused on the attractive face and tried to place her. "I'm sorry…" he said helplessly.

"Michelle Dennis. You used to date my friend, Renee McDonald."

Recognition popped in his eyes. "Wow." He shook his head in embarrassment. "I'm sorry. Spaced out for a minute. How are you?"

"I'm great. Doing a little moonlighting," she said with a smile, giving an expansive look around.

"You were modeling, if I remember correctly."

She laughed a sweet sound. "That, too. In my real life I work at the post office. So how have you been? I think the last time I saw you was about two years ago."

"I've been doing well. Business is booming. Can't complain."

"That's a good thing."

"How's Renee?"

"Renee is married and working on her second baby."

Steven let out a burst of surprised laughter. "You're kidding. Renee?"

"Yep." She bobbed her head.

"'Scuse me, can I get a little service down here?" a man called out from the other end of the bar.

Michelle made a face. "Sorry. Be right back."

Steven took a brief look around. For the middle of the week, the place was fairly crowded with a combination of the straggling after-work patrons and the locals stopping in.

It had been a while since he'd been out alone at a bar. Since he and Mia had gotten together, he'd shut down that part of his life. Funny how a bar was the first place he'd ventured to. He supposed old habits die hard.

Michelle returned. "So what brings you out?" she continued as if they'd never been interrupted.

He shrugged slightly. "Needed some air."

She leaned forward, exposing ample cleavage that Steven could hardly ignore.

She lowered her voice. "Unfortunately, if you're going to sit here, you have to order something. If you don't, my boss will kill me."

"Sure. No problem. I'll take a Coors."

"Coming right up." She turned and bent into the fridge to retrieve the bottle, giving Steven a good solid look from the back. She turned and set the bottle down in front of him, along with a glass and a napkin. "Out for some air, huh?"

He looked at her. When he and Renee had been together he'd seen Michelle several times. She'd always been with a guy, so he hadn't paid much attention to her. Now he did. She was a good-looking woman. Not necessarily a showstopper, but there was something appealing and sexy in her open expression, engaging smile and inviting eyes.

She wore her hair natural in short spirals that took years off her age—middle to late thirties—and her skin looked soft and supple to the touch, with a body that you wouldn't toss out of bed.

"Something like that," he finally said, responding to her question. He took a swallow of the icy-cold beer. "How many nights do you work here?"

"Just two and every other weekend. Helps keep the bills at bay." Her gaze drifted over him. "I get off at ten." She turned and walked a few paces away to serve a customer. She tossed Steven a last look.

Steven looked up the overhead clock above the bar. Ten. He could keep himself occupied until then. Maybe a diversion was just the thing he needed to get his head right. He sipped his beer and relaxed to the music.

Mia had her laptop open on the bed. She'd connected it to her PDA and logged in using the TLC access codes. Within minutes a string of programs opened. She keyed in the necessary information and soon she was inside Michael's office computer.

She did a cursory search of his files and didn't find anything that struck her as out of place, which could mean that there was nothing for her to find or that she would have to open each and every file.

However, after considering her options she thought that if Michael was involved in the escort business, he would minimize any trail from his office. More than likely anything incriminating would be on his home computer or gathered from her phone taps. But if he was using company funds to pay people, there might be something in these files.

She took a second look at a folder labeled Accounts and opened it. At least one hundred files filled the screen. She groaned and began looking at them. The majority of them were businesses, many of which she was familiar with, at least by name. Others were for individuals. As she took one last look, a file marked Log caught her attention. She clicked on the file and a message opened requesting a password. Her heart thumped.

Password. During her training, Jasmine, the head IT person at TLC, had been very clear about passwords. *If you weren't certain that you knew it like your own name, do not try to access the information. If the file is somehow encrypted, then whoever did it would know if attempts had been made to hack into the file.* In cases like that, Jasmine was to be contacted.

Maybe it was nothing, Mia tried to convince herself as she stared at the flashing request for a password. She was probably jumping the gun. Most likely this file was no more than an employee list, or his personal banking information.

What if it wasn't? Was she trying to blow it off because she really believed it was nothing or because she *wanted* to believe it was nothing?

Reluctantly, she picked up her cell phone and dialed TLC headquarters. An automated service answered.

"Welcome to Tender Loving Care beauty products for today's woman. Please enter your ID number now."

Mia pressed in her ID.

"Thank you. If you know your party's extension, please dial it now. To order supplies, press 1; to schedule training, press 2; technical support, press 3. If this is an emergency, please enter your emergency code."

Mia pressed "3."

"Jasmine speaking."

"Hey, Jazz. I have something that I need you to look at. It's encrypted and needs a password."

Jasmine laughed. "Piece of cake. Send me the file."

"Actually I can't. I'm in the subject's computer remotely."

"Go head, girl! Okay. I'm going to take over your computer. Give me your IP address."

Mia did as instructed and seconds later she watched her cursor move around the screen, open and close files and type in strings of code. For an instant the screen went black. When it came back on, Mia was looking at some sort of client list with payment schedules and amounts. All the names were women.

Mia began to feel ill.

"I'm going to take a screenshot of this and e-mail it to you, close the file and then I'll release your computer back to you," Jasmine was saying through the cell phone's speaker. "Got everything you need?"

"Yes, thanks," she said absently.

"Well, good night."

"Night." Mia disconnected the call.

Moments later her computer beeped, indicating a new arrival. She clicked on her in-box and saw the e-mail from Jasmine. She forwarded the e-mail to her office account. She'd print it out there.

Little by little she shut everything down, trying to put a positive spin on what she'd seen.

After putting everything away, she realized how late it had gotten. It was nearing midnight and Steven had yet to return. The fact that he wasn't home was bad enough, but what was more damning was that she hadn't noticed until now.

Steven waited for Michelle to finish her shift. Good sense dictated that he should simply get up and leave. But old habits kicked in and he hung around. He needed some positive re-inforcement and his gut instinct told him that Michelle would be more than willing to do just that.

"Finally," she breathed, coming up to the table where he'd been relaxing for the past hour.

Steven glanced up from his drink. He pushed up from the seat. "I know it's late, but have you eaten?"

"I'm starved."

"Come on. There's a great place about three blocks from here. If we hurry we can catch the kitchen before it closes."

"Lead the way."

They walked out into the brisk evening air.

"Getting cold," Michelle said, pulling her short jacket tighter around her. She slipped her arm through the crook of Steven's and moved closer to him.

"We can take my car if you want."

"No. The air will do me good. I've been cooped up in there for four hours." She walked next to him quietly for about a block. "So tell me what's been going on with you."

A half smile moved across his mouth. "Business has been great. We've expanded some of our developments out to D.C.—"

"That's not what I mean," she said, cutting him off.

He glanced at her.

"I could run an Internet search on you if I wanted to know about your business life."

He chuckled.

"Men don't usually come into a bar alone unless they're looking to meet someone or they have something heavy on their minds. What's your story?"

"Is this the counseling bartender talking?" he teased, avoiding the question.

"No. Just someone who's interested in knowing why a brother like you is out alone at a bar in the middle of the week."

"Maybe I needed a change of scenery."

Michelle stopped walking. Steven stopped short and faced her.

"What?"

Michelle glanced downward then looked him in the eyes. "I want to be honest with you and I hope you'll be honest with me. I like you. I always did, from back when you were dating Renee. But I would never move on my friend's man." She drew in a long breath. "But Renee is married. I'm not seeing anyone and you're out alone."

When he looked at her and took in what she was saying, what she was offering, he had a sudden, sick sensation of guilt. What the hell was he doing? He wasn't that guy anymore. He wasn't on the prowl. He didn't want to retreat to the days when he called all women "sweetheart" because he didn't care or couldn't remember their name.

Had this been a year ago, he probably would have taken Michelle up on her offer.

"Look. It's only dinner with an old acquaintance. Nothing more. If I gave you that impression then I'm sorry."

She pressed her lips together and smiled. "Now that we're on the same page, let's go before the kitchen closes."

Chapter 11

Mia wasn't sure if she should pretend to be asleep when she heard the key in the door or if she should let him know that she was up and was concerned about where he'd been. She peeked at the digital clock. It was nearly 2:00 a.m.

The bedroom door opened. Steven moved quietly around the room, taking off his clothes before going into the master bathroom.

Moments later, Mia heard the shower water running. She stared up at the ceiling. She tried to regulate her breathing and slow down the beating of her heart. This was a new place that she and Steven had entered. Since they'd been together, they'd never been out for most of the night separately. They'd never walked out on each other with friction hovering between them.

She knew part of it was her fault—the secret she was carrying around with her about her conflicting feelings about Michael, and her TLC assignment. She had to get a handle on it before things got worse between them.

The bathroom door opened. For a moment, Steven stood in the lighted doorway before turning off the light.

Mia felt the side of the bed sink from his weight and the covers shift as he got in beside her.

Steven turned on his side and draped his arm across her waist. He kissed her ear. "I know you're not sleeping," he said softly. "Can we talk?"

"Okay," she said softly, while trying to keep her own guilty thoughts from giving her away.

"Something almost happened tonight."

Her heart slammed in her chest. Then Steven was silent for so long she began to believe that her punishment for her own indiscretions was to never know what Steven had "almost" done.

"Look," he finally said. "This whole baring my soul thing is not me. It never has been. But what happened tonight— that can't go on between us."

She was too afraid to move, to breathe.

"I walked out of here tonight because I didn't want you to lie to me anymore."

Oh, God, she was going to faint.

"Are you seeing someone else?"

Her relief burst from her lips. "No! Of course not." She turned on her side to face him. "I wouldn't do that. Never."

From the dim light of the moon sliding in between the blinds, she saw the worry in those incredible eyes, felt it in the rapid beat of his heart and heard it in between the words he did not say; he loved her and was afraid he was losing her. What could she say to prove him wrong when she felt deep in her soul that he might be right—losing her to memories, possibility and unanswered questions.

What she wanted from Steven, she suddenly realized, was more than great sex, nice things and a guaranteed date on Saturday night. She wanted a man who was willing to give every ounce of himself to her, who wanted her so much that he was willing to build a house for her even if they weren't together. She wanted someone to say the words *I love you, Mia* without the prompts, without it only coming as an echo of her own words.

"When things get so that they're not working for you, you need to tell me," Steven was saying, drawing her back and away from her cascading thoughts.

"I can't imagine that happening." But fear and doubt knotted her stomach. She cuddled closer. He tenderly kissed the top of her head. "You want to tell me what almost happened?" she tentatively asked.

"It didn't. That's what's important. Didn't come close, only the suggestion—if I'd been willing."

Mia listened intently for words between the lines and beneath the surface. She found none. Only the simple truth.

Mia gently draped her leg over his. Their toes touched and played. She smiled inside.

Steven pressed his lips against the sensitive spot between the space of her neck and her collarbone. She trembled. He ran his hand down and along the curve of her body's right side, covering each inch like the brush of a master painter.

Mia spontaneously arched her body into his. The pulse of his growing erection pressed between the juncture of her thighs. She moaned softly as he brushed his thumb across her nipple before cupping her breast in his palm and caressing it. Her body became infused with heat.

Steven eased her onto her back. He stared down into her eyes. He looked as if he was on the verge of saying something. Instead he kissed her long, deep and slow. And she gave in to the kiss, the feel of his hands on her body, the weight of him pinning her beneath him.

Mia closed her eyes, wrapped her arms and legs around Steven and let the sensations take over her mind, body and soul.

* * *

The following morning after Steven left for work, Mia set up the tools of her trade and spent the next hour watching the computer screen for activity and listening to the phone taps for something worthwhile.

Just as she was about to pack up and head to the office, Michael received a call on his Sag Harbor phone.

She sat up straighter.

"Hi, it's Michelle. I need some extra hours. Slot me in for any upcoming openings. Thanks."

Mia frowned. What did that mean? Was Michelle one of the alleged women in the service or nothing more sinister than an employee who needed some O/T or the cleaning lady?

She looked at the incoming call for the number. It read like a cell phone. She made a note to give it to Jasmine to see if she could get a last name and maybe an address.

Mia checked the time. It was nearly ten. She needed to stop by the cleaners on her way to work and drop off a few things. She had a conference call at noon.

She put everything away, shut off the computer and stashed her PDA and cell in her tote, along with her go bag. She collected the clothes that she'd tossed on the side chair in the bedroom. She added the two pairs of slacks and a dress shirt that Steven had hung on the back of the bathroom door.

One last look around to ensure that she hadn't left any telltale signs of her clandestine activity and she hurried out.

"Good morning, Ms. Carol," Mia greeted her.

Carol Bennett was the matriarch of the Bennett Dry Cleaning family. Mia had been bringing her clothes to them for years. And although there was a more modern cleaner closer to her condo, she preferred the personal touch, and it gave her a sense of pride to support a black-owned business.

"Mia, how are you, sweetheart?" Carol slipped on the glasses held around her neck by a beaded chain.

"I'm fine, Ms. Carol. How is the family?"

"The children—" she shrugged "—they wish they had a different business to inherit. But it's like I tell them all the time—baby doctors, morticians and cleaners will always have business."

Mia chuckled. "You are so right."

Carol held up each garment and jotted them down on the slip. "Okay, one ladies' suit, two blouses, two dress shirts and two slacks. When do you need them back?" She peered at Mia from above the top of her glasses.

"Hmm. Tomorrow? Can I pick them up around six?"

"Sure."

"Great. Thanks. I gotta run. Have a good day." She picked up her purse from the counter.

"You, too, dear." She gathered the clothes up into a bundle with the intention of putting them in the basket when some change fell out of one of the pockets.

Mia stopped. "I'm sorry. I should have checked the pockets."

Carol picked up the change from the floor. "A whole sixty-two cents," she said with a smile. "Not enough to retire on, so you keep it."

Mia grinned. "Thanks."

Carol went through each item to check the pockets. "This is yours, too." She gave her a business card.

Mia took it and stuck it into her tote.

"That's it," Carol concluded.

"Good. If anything else turns up, just leave it with the clothes. Bye!" She hurried out. Hopefully, she wouldn't get caught in traffic. She probably should have left home sooner, but she'd let her quest for answers—or vindication—consume her morning.

Once behind the wheel of her car, she dug her cell phone out of her tote and gave the voice command to call Ashley.

"Hey, Ashley," she said through the speakerphone. "I'm running behind schedule. Hopefully, I should be there in about forty minutes."

"No problem. I have everything covered."

"Any calls?"

"Just one." Ashley paused. "Michael Burke. He plans to stop by later."

Mia's brakes squealed as she nearly rear-ended the driver in front of her. She had about ten seconds to pull herself together before the cars behind her demanded her head on a platter for holding them up.

"Thanks," she managed, easing her foot off the brake and onto the gas. "Did he say what time?"

"I told him we had an early-afternoon appointment. He said it would be around 2:30. He had some information on the event that he wanted to deliver personally."

Mia's heart skipped a beat. "Okay. I'll see you soon." She pressed the speakerphone button and disconnected the call.

What could he have to bring that he hadn't turned over already? Ideally, she wanted to limit her face time with Michael to the bare minimum. Obviously, he had other ideas.

Chapter 12

Michael strolled into his suite of offices, feeling better than he'd felt in months. Since connecting with Mia again, his life seemed to take on a new purpose. He wanted more than the next big contract, a fatter bank account, more houses and more cars than he could live in or drive.

When Mia had left him, he had fallen apart, piece by piece, with the final straw being his divorce. He'd fallen into an abyss of not caring, of only wanting women in his life whom he could control. He drew a macabre pleasure out of getting them to do what he wanted when he wanted. But after five years, he'd grown even more restless. Nothing satisfied him. Not women, clients or money. And then the opportunity to get back in Mia's life presented itself and the dark world into which he'd descended suddenly grew brighter. He walked down the hallway toward his office.

"Good morning, Michael," Brenda greeted him, as she stepped out of her office into the corridor.

"Morning."

She quickly looked right then left. "I thought you were going to call me last night," she said in a hard whisper.

"Not now, Brenda."

She flashed him a tight look, her mouth turning into a single line. "Then when?"

"I'll let you know. Do you have details on the Chrysler account?"

She lifted her chin, unwilling to take the verbal smack he'd given her. "On your desk."

"Thanks." He continued toward his office, certain that if Brenda had daggers they'd be deep in his back. He opened the door to his office, then shut it behind him. He took off his navy-blue Armani jacket and hung it on the rack by the window.

For a moment he stared out onto the street below. Cars, trucks, buses and strings of yellow cabs filled the blacktop. Harried businesspeople darted around a casual slow-strolling, camera-toting tourist.

This was his city. The pulse and rhythm of it beat in his veins like nourishment, but he'd let it all go to get Mia back.

He slung his hands into his pants pockets. Of course, it wouldn't be easy. There were many people who depended on him. He'd miss the excitement, the challenge, the danger and especially the money. But he'd do it for her. If she'd only give him the slightest indication that she still had feelings for him.

He sighed heavily and turned from the window. Before he got that far, there were still a lot of things he was going to have to settle and exorcise from his life. One of them was Brenda.

It was a mistake taking the boardroom into the bedroom. He knew it the moment he'd reserved the hotel suite at the Ritz Carlton. But his wounds were so deep after losing Mia, then his marriage and the endless series of faceless women, that the comfort Brenda offered was what he needed.

They'd fallen into a discreet routine, talking by phone in

the evening, meeting for the weekend at his house in Mont-clair, New Jersey, or for short getaways to Vegas, the Ba-hamas, the Poconos and even the West Coast, on occasion.

The relationship worked for both of them. At least Michael thought it did. The scene that Brenda had put on after the meeting with Mia and Ashley was worthy of YouTube.

She'd stormed into his office, her eyes full of fire, and marched straight up to his desk.

"What is going on between you and her?"

"I don't know what you're talking about."

"Like hell you don't! I saw how you look at her. I hear how you talk to her. It's more than business. Don't BS me." Her chest heaved in and out as her agitation grew. "I love you, Michael. You're not going to do this to me."

It took everything he had to control his rising temper. Had they been in a more private setting, things would have been entirely different. When his dark, brooding gaze pinned her, he saw her involuntary withdrawal, the moment of alarm that widened her eyes.

His tone was bitter cold. "I suggest that you leave my office. Please."

She opened her mouth to speak. He held up his hand to stop her.

"Leave, Brenda, for both our sakes. We'll talk later."

The bluster with which she'd barged in had dwindled to a barely noticeable breeze.

She straightened her shoulders, then turned and walked out.

He'd said they would talk. But the truth was he really didn't want to deal with her. She'd crossed the invisible line by telling him she was in love with him. Love couldn't work between them. Ever.

He cared for Brenda. But he wasn't in love with her and never would be. He released a long, slow breath. He had to handle this delicately. She didn't deserve to be hurt, but he certainly had no intention of ruining this chance with Mia.

Mia got through her morning working hard to keep thoughts of Michael at bay. But what concerned her most was her on-the-fence feelings about Steven.

Before Michael reappeared, she'd been so certain that Steven was "the one." Now she was filled with doubt.

The chirping of her cell phone drew her attention. She looked around for it on top of her desk to no avail. The chirp continued and she realized it was still in her tote.

She hurried across the room to her bag, which was on the side table, reached inside, turning the bag over in the process. "Dammit." She retrieved the phone from the floor just as it stopped ringing and went to voice mail. "Double dammit." She bent down and picked up her belongings from the floor and was in the process of sticking an errant business card in her wallet when she stopped. Frowned.

Last Call Bar & Grill. The address was on Pier 23. Hmm. She didn't recall ever having been there. And her business hinged on her knowing about the businesses in the city to best serve her clients. She flipped the card over and her heart felt as if it actually stopped.

Michelle Dennis. She stared at the number, unable or un-willing to let the numbers make sense. But she couldn't deny what was right in front of her. It was the same number that had showed up on Michael's phone. The same first name—Michelle. She knew this wasn't one of her business cards. It must have fallen out of Steven's pocket at the cleaner. This was where he'd been last night. This was what "almost happened."

Her stomach rolled.

What the hell did it mean? Was this some ugly coinci-dence? God, how was Steven involved? Was he seeing some woman who might be part of this escort service?

Mia was suddenly so hot she couldn't breathe. The implications of what might be going on she didn't want to think about.

Then pushing its way past the suspicions, the doubts and fears was a surge of jealousy that shook her with its intensity. How far did things really go between Steven and Michelle? How long had he known her? Was she someone from his past?

Her gaze shifted to the neatly written name and phone number.

Mia, Ms. Organized, Ms. Anal-Compulsive, felt like she was coming apart. She couldn't focus on anything beyond calling that number and demanding to know who Michelle Dennis was and what she had to do with Steven.

Mia reached for the phone, just as it rang in her hand.

"Your conference call is on line two," Ashley said.

Mia's hand shook. The room came back into focus. What in the world was she getting ready to do—"go hood" on this Michelle? She'd never argued or fought over a man in her life. What was wrong with her?

"Mia?"

She breathed deeply. "Thanks."

"You okay?"

"Yes, I'm fine. I'll, uh, take the call." Focusing on business would help to clear her head and get her thoughts back on track. She pressed the flashing light on the telephone base.

"Sharlene, hi… Yes, we're in the final stages of the plan…"

Fortunately, the conversation was with a client she'd worked with on an annual basis because, as hard as she tried, she really hadn't been paying attention.

Steven. Michael. Steven. How were they connected?

Ashley knocked lightly on the door and stuck her head in. "Got a minute?"

"Sure."

Ashley came in. She stood in front of Mia's desk. "I

wanted to know if you need me to be here when Michael comes."

Mia's gaze rose slowly and settled on Ashley. "Would you?" she asked and her voice broke. Her eyes filled.

Ashley came around the desk and knelt down beside Mia. "What is it? What happened?"

Mia was incredibly torn. She desperately needed to unburden herself. Normally she would tell Savannah or Danielle. But they knew nothing about Michael, and Ashley didn't know about the Cartel. And Mia was trapped in the middle.

What she needed was an ally. She needed someone she could depend on. She tugged on her bottom lip with her teeth. It was wrong. It went against her promise and it could very well put an innocent person in danger.

But protocol had been broken more than a year ago when Savannah made up her own rules and involved her and Danielle. Mia was about to break it again.

"I think you should sit down…"

About a half hour later, Mia had spilled her guts about the Cartel without divulging its location or naming names. She told Ashley about her assignment, the card she'd found and her confusion about what to do next.

Mia sat back, emotionally spent, expecting to hear words of disbelief, laughter, something. She got none of those. What she got was an expression on Ashley's face that she'd never seen before—hard, piercing, no-nonsense. And she instantly knew she'd made the biggest mistake of her life.

"I'm not really from Los Angeles. I'm from D.C."

Mia frowned.

"I didn't just happen to be the lucky one to fill the job opening as your assistant. I was sent here."

Mia pushed her chair back a bit. Her gaze darted toward

her tote. In her go bag the sample-size "body mist" was a bottle of mace. If she could get to it…

"I was sent by the D.C. office when I asked to be relocated."

Mia blinked several times. Ashley was out of focus. What the hell was she talking about?

"I was assigned to be here, by Jean."

Oh…triple damn.

Chapter 13

Mia had every intention of saying something, but she couldn't find the words. Ashley was one of the Cartel operatives? Right under her nose? What kind of member was she if she couldn't spot one of her own right in front of her face, day in and day out?

Then again, that was the whole point of being part of the Cartel. They were all regular, everyday women who could blend in and not draw attention to themselves.

"All the new recruits with less than two full years under their belt have a shadow," Ashley was saying. "Even if they don't know about it. I'm sure you remember what happened with your friend Danielle. Bernard was her shadow."

Yes, Mia remembered. Danielle had been assigned an identity theft job and, shock of shocks, Bernard Hassell, Savannah's stepfather-in-law-to-be was an agent for Homeland Security and a personal friend of Jean's. He wound up being Danielle's shadow, and it was with his help that they were able to bring down the ring that had stolen hundreds of identities and millions of dollars.

"I still can't wrap my mind around the fact that you've been a part of TLC and I never suspected."

Ashley smiled. "Then I guess I'm pretty good, huh?"

"So how badly have I been doing?"

Ashley settled into her seat. "Not bad at all. I will tell you this. Jean knows everything. Don't think for a moment that she didn't know that you and Michael Burke had a past. It's the main reason she selected you for this assignment. If his hands are dirty, he would never suspect that you were the one who was going to clean them."

A sick sensation rolled through her stomach.

"That's why it was more important than ever that you have a shadow—to prevent you from compromising the assignment."

Mia's throat tightened. "So all that pretending to be my friend, listening to all my personal…stuff…it was just all part of the job, too, I suppose."

Ashley's stern expression slowly softened to the one that Mia recognized. She leaned slightly forward. "No. I listened and advised because underneath all this spy stuff, I really like you. I want us to be friends. And everything I told you about me, it was real." The right corner of her mouth lifted to a hopeful smile.

Mia breathed a bit freer. "So now what?"

Ashley straightened. "This is your case. I'm only here to help, not direct. You tell me what you want me to do. That's how this is going to work. I have no intention of taking over."

"Then I guess, since we're on the same side, I should bring you up-to-date on everything I have so far."

They spent the next half hour going over what Mia had recorded from Michael's home and the information she'd accessed on his office computer. And Jasmine, over at tech support, was able to download the list of names and payments that Mia had found on his office computer. She pulled up the information she'd stored on her PDA and shared it with Ashley.

"Pretty impressive set of names and numbers," Ashley said, studying the list.

"Exactly. But to give him the benefit of the doubt, he is a businessman and his business is to know people, make deals and make money in the process."

Ashley flashed Mia a sharp look. "Do you really believe that's what this list is or is it what you want to believe?"

Mia flinched. "I guess a bit of both," she quietly conceded.

"I can't impress upon you enough the importance of separating your feelings from the reality of what is going on. If you don't, you're going to make some major mistakes that could be very costly…and I don't mean monetarily."

"I know. I can handle this."

"Good. So how do you want to proceed? How can I help? Like I said, I'll be more than happy to take over the project with Avante if that would make it easier for you."

"No." There was a new fierceness in her eyes. "You're right about what you said earlier. He would never suspect me. And that's going to be the key to everything. I can get close to him."

"Okay. This is your show." She checked the clock that hung over the door. "He should be arriving shortly."

Mia's heart thumped. She nodded.

"I'll be up front." Ashley got up to leave.

"Ashley…"

She stopped and turned. "Yes."

"Thanks."

Ashley smiled. "That's what spy friends are for."

"Listen, there is something you can do for me."

"Sure."

Mia explained what she wanted.

"I'll have the info for no later than tomorrow."

Mia nodded.

Mia slumped back in her chair after Ashley left, then covered her face with her hands. She was still in a mild state of shock, although she shouldn't have been. Everyone said that Jean Wallington-Armstrong was a brilliant manipulator and had an uncanny sixth sense about people, not to mention her resources in finding out everything about each and every member of her team. She should have known that if anyone would have an inkling about her and Michael's torrid past, it would be Jean.

That fact made Mia more determined than ever to bring the assignment to a swift and satisfying conclusion, no matter which way it turned out. Certainly a part of her hoped that all the signals about Michael were wrong, but if they weren't, she'd deal with it.

Her intercom buzzed.

"Yes?"

"Mr. Burke is here with his client."

Mia was caught off guard. She hadn't expected him to bring anyone, but that was probably a good thing. They wouldn't have an opportunity to be completely alone. She got up from her desk and walked up front to the small reception and file area.

"Michael."

"Mia, you look great, as always."

She merely smiled in response. Then she directed her attention to his guest and walked toward her. Mia extended her hand. "You must be Raven."

The stunning young woman stuck out her hand and limply shook Mia's. She offered a dazzling smile. And Mia immediately saw why crowds would swoon over her.

Raven was at least twenty, a stunning combination of

Japanese and African-American ancestry, which gave her a sleek, exotic look. She had dark, silky hair that reached her waist, large almond-shaped eyes that curved ever so slightly at the corners, and a body like Halle Berry covered in a butter-smooth caramel complexion. She was about five foot five but she gave the appearance of being much taller.

"Raven, it's a pleasure to meet you. Michael has told me a lot about you, and the Internet is full of stories. Please, have a seat." She waited until Raven and Michael were seated. "Michael told me that you're very shy, which must be very difficult in your business."

"It is. I'm trying to deal with it," she said softly.

"We plan to make this event spectacular and as easy on you as possible." She buzzed Ashley.

"Yes?"

"Would you mind bringing in the details we've worked out so far for Raven's red-carpet event?"

"Sure. I'll be right in."

Several moments later Ashley came in with a thick folder.

"Ashley, this is Raven. Ashley is my event coordinator and is going to be responsible for logistics."

For the next few minutes, Mia explained the layout and how they planned to use video and audio clips throughout the night in lieu of Raven having to be engulfed in the throngs of people. Ashley gave a video presentation, detailing how they were going to lay out the space.

"The highlight of the evening will be your performance, which will happen toward the end of the night. Right after you finish, a limo will be waiting to take you back to your hotel. We are creating the image of untouchable for you and I think it will work. It will keep the media guessing and keep you out of the spotlight." She took a breath. "So what do you think?"

Raven beamed in delight. "I love it."

"Wonderful. We'll work out the final details, get the invitations out, handle the RSVPs and then set up the interior." She turned to Michael. "Any questions?"

"I think you've covered everything." He turned to Raven. "I told you she was the best." He stood. "I'm going to head back to the office. I know you ladies are busy and I...*we* appreciate your time. Mia, I'll be in touch. Good seeing you again, Ashley."

"You, too. I'll walk you both out." She spoke to Mia over her shoulder. "I'm going to take care of that errand. If I get finished in time, I'll be back."

Mia nodded.

She slumped back into her chair. Her day had been exhausting, to say the least, and it wasn't over yet.

While Ashley was on her assignment, Mia made a call to the girls.

Chapter 14

Steven and Blake were closing up shop for the night and walking to their respective cars.

"So how are things going with you and Mia? Ever have that talk?"

Steven shrugged slightly. "Sort of."

"Okay." He dragged out the word. "What does that mean?"

"We talked. I told her how I felt…kind of. I mean, damn, she's my woman. She's supposed to know how I feel."

Blake chuckled. "Listen, my good brotha. Here is a lesson in Women 101. Whatever you think you know, you don't. Did you tell her how you feel, what was bothering you?"

"Yeah…kind of."

"Man." He laughed full out. "You sound like you have communication issues, which equals a brother's biggest downfall, not being able or willing to communicate."

"It's just not me, man. The words are in my head, I feel 'em, I just can't get them to cross my lips." He chuckled without humor. "But she has to know how I feel about her. Would I have given up my carefree life, my own crib, if I didn't want to be with her?"

"I know to you it seems obvious. But a woman doesn't always see the surface things. She needs to feel it, she needs to hear it."

Steven blew out a long breath. "I did ask her if she was seeing anyone."

"What did she say?"

"She said no."

"Did you believe her?"

He hesitated for a moment. "Yeah."

"Well, that's something. A start. You just have to talk to her, man. Once you get started, it gets easy. I swear." He grinned, seeing the pained looked on his friend's face. He slapped him on the back.

"I almost hooked up with this woman I met the other night."

Blake stopped in his tracks. "Say what?"

"I don't know. I was angry, confused, so I went for a drive and found myself out by Chelsea Piers. Stopped in this bar and grill. Remember when I was dating Renee McDonald?"

"Vaguely. They were coming and going so fast and furious it was hard to keep up," he teased.

"Very funny. Anyway, she had this friend, Michelle Dennis. Well, that's who I ran into the other night—Michelle. She was working the bar."

Blake's brows rose. "And…"

"And she made it clear that if I was willing, so was she."

Blake lowered his head and shook it slowly. "But good sense prevailed…"

"Yeah, that's not what I'm looking for. I'm not on the prowl anymore, don't want to be."

"Hey, none of us can afford to be. Black folk have the

highest rates of HIV/AIDS and the numbers aren't coming down. These days you play, you pay, and it could be with your life. It ain't worth it, man."

"Humph, who you telling? I had my scare just before I met Mia. Don't plan to go down that road again."

"So where are things with you and Mia? You two on the same page or what?"

"I think so, man. I know I have work to do. It's just gonna take some time."

Blake draped his arm around Steven's broad shoulders as they walked across the underground parking lot. He leaned close. "If it's in your heart, man, just say the words." He grinned. "It feels almost as good as great sex."

Steven chuckled. "Yeah, okay."

They parted ways and Steven got in his car and sat there for a few moments as he watched Blake drive off.

Tonight he'd make a special effort. He'd show Mia how much he cared.

When he arrived at their condo, Mia hadn't gotten in yet. It was a little after six, plenty of time to plan a romantic evening in New York.

He walked into the bedroom, tossed his briefcase and jacket onto the lounge chair then went to the phone by the bed.

He knew it was too last minute for any of the high-end restaurants in the area, but there was a local Italian place, totally family-owned, that Mia swore by. He placed an order with special instructions for delivery.

With that task out of the way, he went in search of some candles. In moments, the air was filled with the soft scent of vanilla. Mia's favorite. He checked the time. If Mia stayed true to form, she should be getting in between eight and nine, although lately it had been closer to nine. That gave him close to two hours to find the right music, break out the special dinnerware, put the chocolate-colored satin sheets on the bed and still have time to run out for some flowers and take a shower before she got home.

Steven smiled as his plans for the evening began to take shape. He may not say the right words all the time, but he knew how to put on a grand party.

Mia was the first to arrive at The Shop. The trio—Savannah, Danielle and she—had been coming to the little West Village bistro for years, Mia having discovered it during one of her canvassing jaunts of the city in search of venues for clients or possible events. She was so pleased with the atmosphere, the service and the food that she made it a permanent stop and the girls adopted it as well.

She secured their booth in the back. By the time she got settled, she looked up and Danielle, stunning as always in an exotic kind of way, was walking through the door, with Savannah, still holding on to the lush postbaby curves, right behind her.

The moment Mia saw her two dearest friends walking through the door, the tightness that had lived in the center of her stomach for days and days began to ease. These were her girls, her friends. She needed them now more than ever, but if they were to be in any kind of position to help her, she would first have to come clean. She drew in a long breath of resolve and let out a breath of determination.

"Hey, girl," Danielle greeted her, buzzing Mia's cheek with a light kiss.

"My turn," Savannah said, the glow of happiness brimming in her eyes as she followed Danielle's greeting.

They both settled down into the worn leather booth seats.

"Dinner on you," Danielle asked, "since you convened this soiree?"

"Sure, and drinks, too."

Savannah's wide brown eyes widened even farther. "Must be serious with you springing for dinner *and* drinks. Do I need mine now?"

Mia's expression pinched for a moment. "You might."

Danielle raised her hand to signal for the waitress. "I'll have a cosmo," she said upon the waitress's arrival.

Savannah ordered a daiquiri and Mia an apple martini.

"So what's up, sis?" Savannah said. "I don't think I can wait for drinks." She lowered her voice. "Is it about your assignment?"

"Partly."

Danielle and Savannah leaned closer, their expressions open and expectant.

"I don't even know where to begin," Mia said.

"Wherever you feel comfortable," Savannah offered in that soft way of hers.

Mia lowered her gaze, trying to organize her thoughts. She looked into the eyes of her friends. "I've never told either of you this before. For that I apologize, but I think after I tell you everything you'll understand why. At least I hope you will." She swallowed. "When Jean gave me the assignment, it wound up being about investigating someone I knew…intimately…"

Mia poured out her story, from her shock at finding out that Michael was the suspect of the investigation, then traveling back to how they'd met, their torrid affair, his being married, him being her first true love, the guilt she felt about their affair, the breakup. She told it all: her visit to his house in Sag Harbor, the one he said he'd had built with her in mind, her growing feelings of uncertainty about her and Steven. She told them everything—up to and including the fact that Ashley was a Cartel operative and was at the moment tracking down Michelle Dennis.

By the time she'd finished, they'd consumed two drinks each and their dinner was halfway eaten. During the entire time, neither Danielle nor Savannah said a word.

Mia sat back, looked from one stunned face to the other, waiting for the verdict.

"You could have told me," Savannah said, surprising Mia. She thought Savannah would have been appalled that Mia would have taken up with a married man. "I know I might come across as all straight-laced and whatnot, but those are *my* rules. I don't put them on anyone else, especially my friends. Love comes in all kinds of packages and at all different times. I may not agree with what you did, but I admire how you finally took care of it." She reached across the table and took Mia's hand, which was balled into a fist.

"Girl, I would never have thought you had it in you," Danielle said with her usual sarcasm. "But the real deal is not what happened then, but what is happening now. Do you still have feelings for him?"

"That's just it. I don't know. I'm not sure if the feelings are real or some kind of residue of the past."

"You know you have to get that together," Savannah said. "First, for the sake of your relationship with Steven and then for the Cartel. We both know what it's like trying to manage a relationship and these assignments. We've been there."

Danielle wholeheartedly agreed. "And so Ms. Girl is a TLC lady." Danielle grinned. "I knew I liked her."

"Jean is something," Savannah said. "It's really kinda scary how much she knows and how she puts people exactly where they need to be. She knew it was going to be Blake's company that would be involved with the Tristan Montgomery investigation, and she knew that Dani and Nick's relationship was going to be put to the test with her identity theft assignment."

"She puts us in these kinds of emotional tugs-of-war situations to test our loyalty to the organization," Danielle said. "I guess when she realizes that we won't compromise ourselves, our relationships or the organization, we are truly Cartel-worthy."

Savannah lifted her glass then put it back down. "Can I just say this? I've seen you and Steven together. I see how he looks at you and how you look at him. I hear how you talk about him—the joy in your voice." She took a breath. "One thing I've learned is that you can't go back. If Michael could cheat on his wife, what makes you think that if it was just the two of you he wouldn't wind up doing the same thing to you?"

"And bottom line," Danielle cut it. "If he's under suspicion by Jean and the Cartel and you have come up with your own suspicions, chances are there's something to it, sis. If you're going to hinge old feelings onto this assignment, you'll never see clearly and it could really get you hurt in more ways than one."

"I don't know Michael," Savannah said gently. "But if you loved him, I'm sure at his core he is a decent man. You are the only one who can make the right decision. You know your heart and you know both of them. I know that you'll do what is best for everyone involved, because I know *you*."

"Exactly, sweetie. We love you and don't want to see you hurt, but you know we got your back no matter what choice you make," Danielle added.

Mia sniffed back tears of relief. These were her friends, her sisters in spirit through good and bad, and she should have known that they would understand and not judge her. Such a weight had been lifted from her soul after finally being able to share with them what she had been through and the situation she currently found herself in.

And, like the dear friends and fellow Cartel members they were, they were willing to help with the case in any way that they could.

* * *

As she drove home, Mia thought about everything that was said during their impromptu get-together. Of course they were right. Deep in her soul it was something she already knew. She could not remain torn. Too much was at stake, specifically her relationship with Steven.

Her heart twisted just a little in her chest. She was being so unfair. She'd begun to compare Steven to Michael. That wasn't right. They were two different kinds of people and they showed their affection in different ways. Simply because Steven didn't shower her with words of love did not mean that he didn't love her. He *showed* her how he felt.

No more sitting on the fence. No more questioning her feelings and her relationship. She pulled into a parking space across the street from her condo. She loved Steven. True, she'd loved Michael, deeply. But *loved* was the operative word. *Past tense*. She must live in the now. And that was exactly what she intended to do.

When she put her key in the door, the soft scent of vanilla wafted to her nose. The living room was dim, apparently illuminated by candlelight.

Slowly she put down her purse on the hall table and closed the door. She distinctly heard the Luther Vandross classic "A House is Not a Home," crooning softly in the background. What was going on? And was that veal parmesan she smelled?

"Steve? Honey…I'm home," she said, and almost laughed at the oft-used one-liner.

Steven emerged from the bedroom, clad only in black silk boxers that hugged his chiseled chocolate skin. Her heart thumped along with the tiny bud between her thighs as he came toward her. Steven held their circular silver serving tray perched up on one hand with two long-stemmed wine glasses filled with something clear and bubbly. He had a white towel draped across his other arm.

"Good evening," he said in a low voice, the inkling of a smile hovering around the corners of his mouth.

Mia moved in closer, her eyes full of questions. That's when she spotted the huge bouquet of flowers in the center of the living-room table, bursting with color.

"What is going on?" she asked with a girlish giggle in her voice.

"You are being served," Steven said. He waved his hand toward the dining area that was an extension of the living room closer to the window. "Please have a seat." He went to the rectangular cherrywood table that sat six, set down the tray and pulled out a chair for her.

She looked up at him as he placed a glass of champagne in front of her. "Whatever you have on your mind, I'm loving it so far."

"That's the plan." He winked then disappeared into the kitchen.

Mia thoughtfully sipped her champagne. What in the world had gotten into Steven? He was always sweet and willing to help out: cook, clean, whatever was needed. But this—even for Steven, this was taking it to the next level.

When she heard his footsteps approaching, she turned toward him and her mouth dropped open. He was rolling in their food cart, laden with piping-hot dishes of veal, linguini, shrimp marinara, hot buttered rolls and steamed vegetables that made her mouth water. Forget the fact that she'd just had a large Caesar salad and two drinks. Suddenly she was starving.

"Dinner is served," he said with a slight bow, bringing the cart to rest next to her. He lifted one of the plates from the tray and placed it in front of her.

She looked across at him as he took a seat opposite her,

and her heart filled with love and lust for her man. "Steven…I'm speechless." Her eyes sparkled and her voice kept getting caught in her throat. "What…a beautiful surprise. I…don't know what to say."

"Don't say anything. Just enjoy." He smiled at her and she saw something in his eyes that she couldn't describe.

She nodded, her lips pressed tightly together to keep from crying.

He'd set the CD player to play all her favorites, from Luther to Kem, Barry White to the Dells, Marvin, Teddy, the Manhattans, some old-time Ella with a little Miles mixed in. Steven was the music aficionado. He could talk about music from every genre and era and not miss a beat, no pun intended. And if he was coaxed enough, he'd even play a little alto sax when they had their get-togethers. Truth be told, he didn't have to be coaxed hard at all.

And that's what he did tonight. Standing right in front of the window, with nothing on but those silk boxers and satin skin, he brought the sax to his lips and blew out a soulful tune that vibrated through her insides, made her want to weep with the purity of the sound, the sweetness of it as he serenaded her.

She wasn't sure how they made it into their bedroom, because the loving started from the moment she'd walked in the door, through dinner and a bubble bath that awaited her, to the satin sheets that they only used on "special occasions."

Steven toyed with and played with her body as expertly as he played the sax, with artistry and precision, awakening every nerve ending until her entire body vibrated and trembled with desire.

When he parted her thighs and tenderly drank of her essence, she knew heaven. The roar and rush of sensations that jettisoned through her made her head spin. Her body was no longer her own. It belonged to him. She knew that. And when he slowly, deliberately, inch by taunting inch, eased deep inside her, tears of exquisite joy seeped from her eyes as they moved to the rhythm that was uniquely their own.

Steven's heart and soul seemed to merge with Mia's. When he was inside her, he felt protected and safe, believing that nothing could ever compare to what he experienced and felt when he was with her.

Women had always been a part of his life, yet more of an afterthought than an integral piece. But Mia was different. Since they'd been together, his world revolved around her, revolved around making her happy. He knew he still had that hard edge, still had that part of him that he was leery of exposing and releasing—his gentle side—the side that his mother nurtured but was beaten back by his father.

But Mia had cracked that door open, pushed it ajar, and he could see possibility on the other side and it scared him with its intensity—the valley of the unknown. Yet he knew deep in his soul that if he dared to cross the threshold, Mia would be there waiting for him on the other side, willing to embrace him so that he would not fall. She'd lead him out of that dark place and into the light of her love.

He felt all those things, one on top of the other as he moved within her and she held him, stroked his back, cried his name, wrapped him in her love.

And suddenly the words burst from his lips as the explosion fired in his belly.

"I love you," he groaned in agony and ecstasy. "I love you."

And when he said the words, the world seemed to open, but maybe it was his heart. The happiness that rushed through him made him dizzy and he shook violently with the force of verbal and physical release.

Mia held him, took him in, rocked him to greater heights and she cooed in his ear, "I know, baby, I know." And she did.

* * *

As they held each other, drifting in and out of the sleep of the totally satiated, Mia heard the distance chime of her cell phone. Whoever it was would have to wait until morning, she thought, drifting deeper into sleep. Her man loved her, and for now that was all that mattered.

Chapter 15

The following morning, after Steven had left for work, Mia busied herself cleaning up from the dinner of the night before, then settled down to her own morning ritual. She'd sent Steven off to work with a Kool-Aid smile on his face, as she'd decided that what was needed to get their morning off on the right foot was a little change of venue.

Before the sun came up, like two kids, they took the elevator of their six-story building up to the top floor and locked it. Then they totally reenacted the elevator scene from *Fatal Attraction*.

Giggling like two teens, they returned to their apartment, to the glaring stares of a couple who'd been waiting for the elevator.

Amused, she thought about that as she checked out Page Six, circled some interesting articles and dug in to her omelet. Just as she was about to take her second bite, she heard the distinctive sound of her cell phone and suddenly remembered the unanswered call from the night before.

She hopped up from her chair and hurried out into the hallway, where she'd left her purse. She dug out her phone. Her heart thumped when she saw Ashley's number come up on the caller ID.

"Hello?"

"Hi, did you get my message?"

"Actually, no. I haven't checked. What did you find out?"

"I think we need to talk in person. What time will you be in the office?"

"I should be there within the hour." Her chest tightened. "How bad is it?"

"Bad enough. Let's just say that by the looks of things, Michael Burke is in deep. I'll see you at the office."

A sick sensation ran through her, souring her stomach. A part of her hoped that all the bad signals that they were getting about Michael would be wrong. She sighed heavily, stared at her omelet, her paper and her gun.

She could no longer push the inevitable aside. She had a job to do, and if Michael got caught up in the net, then so be it.

"It appears that this Michelle Dennis is on the payroll. She may be moonlighting at the bar but she definitely has another sideline," Ashley was saying. "We got to talking while I nursed my drink. I told her that I sure could use some extra income and had been trying to find something. She told me if I was really interested and was willing to be friendly with some really wealthy men from time to time, she might be able to set something up for me."

The more Ashley talked about her meeting with Michelle, the sicker Mia felt.

"I asked her what she meant by *friendly*. She was quick to tell me that you never had to do anything you didn't want to. Mostly it was to be dates for businessmen, make them feel good and important, be seen with them at functions, things like that. And it paid very well. Now it was up to each girl what they were willing to do beyond that.

"Anyway, she gave me a number and told me to give this guy a call. The guy is Michael."

Whatever hope Mia had that this was all some ugly mistake, some strange mixup, was now gone. She nodded solemnly.

"Okay," Mia said on a breath. "Now we know. The next step is to get the goods on him and everyone he works with, and turn it over to Jean."

"Exactly. But I think we're going to need some help. Michael has already met me. No way can I turn up as a potential escort to get behind the scenes."

That much was true. Mia thought about it for a minute. Now that both Savannah and Danielle knew about Michael and were both part of the Cartel, she might be able to call on them for assistance. Especially since Michael had never met either one of them.

"First things first. We have the red-carpet event for Raven. That will be a perfect opportunity to check out everything up close," Mia said.

"Do you really think that he would risk something like that at a major event?"

"I know Michael. The challenge of pulling it off would be enough to make him do it. With the list of who's who in attendance, I can pretty much guarantee that some of his ladies will be there."

"Okay. We start there. Of course, I can't chance being at the party now. If Michelle shows up, we'll have a problem."

That reality struck Mia and momentarily dimmed the light in her eyes.

"As a matter of fact, now that I'm thinking about it, I know she will be there. While we were talking, she mentioned a major event coming up—something to do with some new singer, was the way she put it. She intimated that Michael might be willing to use some extra help."

Mia was thoughtful for a moment. "We'll find a way to work it out. We're not superspies for nothing."

Ashley grinned.

For the next few days it was a constant whirlwind of activity for MT Management. Putting in place all the intricate pieces for hosting this major blowout event took up all their time and energy, not to mention the other clients they had as well.

While Mia tried to stay focused on the red-carpet event, Ashley worked on the boutique grand opening. They barely had enough time to talk to each other in the office, between the phone calls, meetings and endless errands that they had to run in addition to dealing with the long list of vendors for each of the events.

Mia was seriously considering hiring a new assistant because the long hours were really beginning to take a toll. But as Steven had told her over lunch several weeks earlier, the last thing you want to do is hire someone only to find out in six months that you have to let her go. Perhaps she could advertise for a temporary position or just use one of the agencies. At least a temp could take calls and even do some of the running around.

She thought about it as she looked at her computer screen, which displayed the layout of the venue. With her luck she'd probably wind up hiring yet another Cartel member. She chuckled at the thought.

"It's always good to see you laughing."

She jerked up in her seat. Her eyes went to the door.

"Michael. What are you doing here?"

He stepped fully into the office and Mia silently cursed the fact that she didn't have that third hand. Ashley was with the two sisters going over the menu for their opening, which left her alone in the office.

"No one was out front, so I wandered in."

"Wandered in from where? Your office is on the other side of town."

He grinned. "I know, but I suddenly got this overwhelming urge to see you and I couldn't seem to stop myself."

She swallowed over the sudden dry knot in her throat. The sultry, manly scent of him drifted to her nose, short-circuiting her thoughts.

"That's really nice, but I'm so busy."

He came around behind her. She could feel the heat of his body. She held her breath.

He reached over her shoulder and pointed to the screen. "Is that the venue for Raven's event?"

"Yes." Her voice shook. She wanted to get up, but he had her trapped in her chair.

"Michael…I'm really busy…"

His hand drifted down, first resting on her shoulder. Her heart was hammering so hard she could barely breathe. His fingers grazed the top of her right breast and she gasped.

"Don't you remember how it was? Just let me touch you, Mia," he crooned in that tone that always made her do things she shouldn't. "I can make you remember." He cupped her breast in his palm and moved it in a slow circle. She saw stars an instant before reality struck.

She pushed back in her chair with all the force she could summon, making him stumble backward. She leaped up from her seat and whirled toward him. With her back to the desk, she gripped the edge to keep herself from falling as her knees had turned to jelly.

His eyes were dark, hungry and filled with lusty need. Her chest rose up and down in rapid succession as she tried to breathe to clear her head.

"I want you," he groaned. "I want you so badly that I ache every minute of the day. Can't you understand that?" In an instant he was right upon her and with nothing but air to separate them he pressed his body up against hers and she felt his need grind into her.

Oh, God, she remembered.

He snaked his arm around her waist and pinned her to him. "Feel that?" he said against her neck.

Her thoughts were turning like a merry-go-round. Her body was on fire.

Michael reached for the hem of her skirt and pushed it up toward her hips.

"I love you." But it wasn't Michael's voice that she heard. It was Steven's.

His large hand went under her skirt. Reality slammed against her. She grabbed his wrists with all her strength.

"Don't do this, Michael. Don't!"

The front door opened. Michael moved back, looking toward Mia's partially opened office door. Mia pushed down her skirt just as Ashley's voice called out that she was back.

"I need you to leave. Please."

"I'm…I'm sorry. I know I shouldn't have done that." He reached out to her. "I'm sorry."

She pushed his hand away. "Please…"

Ashley tapped on the door and stepped in. All at once she took in the torrid scene. To the untrained eye it would appear harmless enough; Mia leaning slightly against the edge of her desk with Michael looking handsome and oh-so-casual. But beneath the surface the air was hot, the heat of sexual tension so high that it could suffocate you. And if you looked very close, you could see the tiny line of perspiration that ran across Michael's hairline, Mia's quicker-than-normal breathing and a look that almost resembled panic in her eyes.

Ashley's eyes bounced from one to the other. She came

fully into the room. "Good to see you again, Michael. Is everything okay?" She looked to Mia. "With the plans," she qualified.

Mia glanced away for a second. "Yep, Michael was just leaving, actually."

"You ladies are doing a fantastic job. I know it's going to be a great event." He started to move from behind Mia's desk. "She was just showing me the layout of the venue on the computer." He grinned. "Damn computer programs can do just about anything." He headed for the door then stopped, slapped his palm against his forehead. "I almost forgot why I stopped by." He reached into the breast pocket of his jacket and pulled out an envelope with the Avante Enterprises logo on the front. He handed it to Mia. "That's the other portion of your payment. And as we agreed, if it is as successful as I know it's going to be, there'll be a fifteen percent bonus on the total cost." He pulled the door open, stepping past Ashley. "Have a great day, and see you both on Friday." He walked out.

Mia slowly eased herself into her chair.

"Mia, what's going on? What did I almost walk in on?"

"Nothing," she managed to say.

"It didn't look like nothing and it's hot as a sauna in here. Did he try something?"

"No," she lied, because if she admitted the truth, she'd have to admit that she almost let him and she couldn't admit that. She wouldn't. "Nothing more than his usual, let's-get-back-together talk." She forced a smile. "It's fine. Really. How did everything go with the sisters?"

Ashley looked at her and decided to let it go. Mia was a grown woman. Hopefully, she knew what she was doing. But one thing was certain: Ashley was not going to stand by and let Mia screw up this assignment over a man she very well may still have the hots for, a man who was their prime target. Not on her watch.

* * *

Michael returned to his office. What he needed was a cold shower. What had he been thinking? That's just it. He hadn't been thinking, at least not with the head on top of his shoulders. He'd been totally blinded by lust. That wasn't like him. But Mia had that effect on him—she always did. And the years that they'd been apart had not dampened his need for her. If anything, it had intensified. He had to get himself under control before he really blew it. If there was any chance of them getting back together again, what almost happened in her office wasn't the way to make it happen.

His stomach twisted with regret when he remembered the look of fear in her eyes. He would never hurt her. He prayed that she understood that. Somehow he'd find a way to make it up to her.

He continued down the corridor to his office and walked inside. Before he had a chance to get settled, there was a knock on his door.

"Come in." He took off his jacket and tossed it on the back of his chair. He looked up. It was Brenda.

"Hi," she said tentatively. "Can we talk for a minute?"

"Sure. Come in and close the door." He sat down.

Brenda came in and sat opposite him. "I, um, I just want to tell you that I was wrong for flipping out on you the other day. From the beginning you never lied to me about what this relationship was. You never led me on or tried to make me believe that it was more than what it actually was. That's all on me."

"Brenda…look, you don't have to—"

She cut him off. "Please…let me finish before I lose my nerve," she said with a shaky laugh. "I know how I feel about you, Michael, and I accept the fact that you don't feel the same way about me." She lowered her gaze then looked directly at him. "I wish things were different, but they aren't." She drew in a long breath. "So I'm going to back off. If you want to be with someone else, I understand. I won't stand in your way. But if you ever change your mind or things don't work out…well, you have my number." She stood.

For the first time Michael saw Brenda, really saw her for the strong, intelligent, pretty woman that she was. She'd been there for him when he didn't know if he was coming or going. She'd helped run his business when he'd lost all interest. She'd listened to him, she'd counseled him. She loved him purely. And somewhere beneath all the rubble of his emotions, he knew that he truly cared for her. True, not in the way that she wanted and certainly not in the way he felt about Mia. But he cared for her. And the sad part was he'd been so absorbed in himself and his business and making deals and money that he'd never given her the chance to be all that she could be in his life. He'd taken her presence and her body for granted, as if it were some kind of entitlement of his rather than a gift.

Brenda turned to leave and her always proud shoulders were slightly bent, as if she'd been defeated by some unseen force.

"Brenda, wait."

She turned to him. He smiled softly. "How about dinner tonight? It's been a while. We could leave early and go to my place out on the Harbor. What do you say?"

She hesitated. Thought about the implications, what she really wanted and what she knew she could get. She loved him so deeply and so strongly that she'd been willing to settle for whatever he was giving. What kind of half life was that? She deserved more. She was a good woman and she deserved a man who loved her as much as she loved him. And until Michael purged his soul of that woman who'd bewitched him, he could never be that man for her.

"I don't think so, Mike. But thank you for asking." She opened the door, stepped out and closed it softly behind her.

* * *

"I've been thinking about hiring a temp for the office," Mia was saying as she and Ashley finally found time to scarf down a salad and some diet soda. "I was looking at our calendar for the next four months and I truly cannot see how we are going to be able to manage without some help."

"I'd been thinking the same thing. And with the shaky economy, temp is definitely the way to go."

"Would you mind checking with a few of the agencies and see if they can send some potential candidates over?"

"Sure. Not a problem. I'll take care of it right after lunch. Listen, have you thought any more about what you want me to do about this Michelle chick and the phone call that I have yet to make to Michael?"

Mia took a swallow of her soda. "Yes, and I've tossed ideas around in my head. I was thinking that we're going to have to bring in some help. You can't be on scene Friday night. I'm going to ask Savannah and Danielle to step in."

"Makes sense. Have you talked with them yet?"

She thought about the confession she'd made to her two best friends the night before. A soft smile framed her mouth. "Yes. And I told them everything…finally," she admitted.

Ashley nodded. "Good. They should know. They're your friends. How did they take it?"

"Much better than I could have ever imagined. They were totally in my corner, as they've always been. I do have to ask them if they're free Friday night," she said, laughing lightly.

"I'm sure they will be." Ashley got up from the small circular conference table in Mia's office and collected the remnants of their lunch. "I'll start making those calls to the temp agencies. If we're lucky, maybe we can get someone before the end of the week."

Ashley turned to walk out just as the front door to the office opened. Both she and Mia's brows rose in unison.

Chapter 16

"Brenda," Ashley said before looking over her shoulder to Mia. "What can we do for you?"

Today was definitely the day for uninvited guests, Mia thought in a rush. She stood up and came toward the door.

"Actually, I came to see Ms. Turner." She looked past Ashley at Mia's approach. "I know I should have called first but I took a chance that you would be here. Do you have a few minutes?"

"Of course. Come in."

"I'll, uh, start making those calls," Ashley said before closing Mia's door.

"Please, sit. What can I help you with? If this is about the event on Friday, everything is taken care of."

"No, it's not the event. As Michael said, he only hires the best, so I'm sure everything is fine." She slipped out of her lightweight coat and draped it across her lap as she sat down. "It's about Michael."

Oh, damn. What now? "Michael?"

"Yes." She paused. "I'm not sure how to even go about this. This is so out of character for me."

Mia waited. Was this going to be one of those *Jerry Springer* episodes?

"I know that Michael is in love with you."

Mia flinched inside.

"And I'm in love with him." She sputtered a laugh. "Unfortunately, he doesn't feel the same way. But I know he cares about me. At least as much as he can." She studied her folded hands then stared Mia straight in the eye. Her expression suddenly hardened. "I know things—things that could ruin him."

Mia's heart started to kick up a notch. Aw, damn, this was the woman-scorned episode.

"I know who you are and what you do."

Mia laughed nervously. "Of course you do."

"That's not what I mean." She reached into her purse and took out a tiny black disk. She placed it solidly down on the table.

Mia nearly had a heart attack. It was the listening device that she'd planted in Michael's office.

"Look familiar?"

Mia frowned, going for her Oscar for best actress. "Haven't got a clue. It looks like a black quarter or something. What is it and why should I care?"

"I've used them before. Plenty of times. It may have been dark in the room while you and Ashley were doing your song-and-dance routine the other day, but I was watching you. I saw you when you placed it under the table. I went back to check after you left. I recognized it right away. I should have dumped it, but I didn't want you getting suspicious about what happened to it. But I thought for the purposes of this meeting I should bring it so that you'd know I wasn't bluffing."

Yep, she was going to have a heart attack. Right this minute and then this nightmare would be over.

"I have no idea what you're talking about."

"Let's not play games, okay? I was a member about eight years ago."

"Member?" she echoed.

"Yes, of the Cartel. I was based in Chicago until I moved here and wanted to get out of the business. That's when I met Michael. Jean Wallington-Armstrong sound familiar?"

This was a test. Jean was obviously up to her tricks again.

"No, it doesn't. And to be honest, I'm really busy, as you know, so please get to the point of your impromptu visit so that I can get back to work."

Brenda dug in her purse again; this time she took out her cell phone. She dialed a number. "Yes, 258643," she said to whomever answered. She kept her gaze on Mia. Moments passed. "Hello, Jean, it's Traci."

Traci?

"I knew if I used my old code all the red flags would go up and it would get you on the line. I'm here with Mia. I think I have information that you can use." She listened before passing the phone back to Mia.

"Hello?"

"Listen to me carefully. Just agree with everything I'm saying."

"Sure, of course."

"I'm going to send Bernard over there right now. Keep her talking. Bernard will bring her in. I'm going to send an alert to Ashley immediately so that she will know what's going on. Subdue her if she tries to leave."

"Great. I understand. Thank you. Yes, I'll check in later." She swallowed and handed the phone back over to Brenda. Mia forced a crooked smile. "Guess you're the real deal. Seems to be raining secret agents lately," she said, more to herself than Brenda or Traci—whatever her name was. "So what is it that you know that you think I should?"

"First of all, I'm not crazy. That's what Jean is going to try to convince you of. I left the Cartel because I couldn't deal with the double life, the havoc that it was wreaking on everything I did. I spent all my time lying to my friends, and in my relationships. I couldn't take it anymore. The thrill, the excitement was gone. I went to Jean and I told her. She tried to make me stay. Said I was the best operative she'd seen in years, but I told her I couldn't do it anymore, I needed a life—a real life." She paused. "So she essentially erased me from existence. Any association that I had with the Cartel was deleted, all traces of my connection to them were removed. You could get the best computer hackers in the world and they'd never be able to find a shred of information on my being part of the Cartel."

Mia got a sudden chill.

"She made me disappear." She glanced away for a moment. "Once I knew that I was finally free, I left Chicago and came here to New York. I got a job with Michael's company as Brenda Forde. Traci Bennett was gone, buried. Until now."

"I can't believe that Jean didn't know you were here, that you worked for Michael."

Brenda smiled smugly. "As I told you in the beginning, even Jean had to admit that I was the best. I wanted to cover my tracks, and I did. She had no idea who I was."

So Jean wasn't infallible after all, Mia thought. She didn't have a sixth sense, at least not in this case. "You still haven't told me what you came here to say."

"Michael has another business, a very secret but lucrative one. He has no idea that I know about it. But simply because I'm no longer a card-carrying member of the Cartel doesn't mean that I've lost my skills." She stared at Mia. "I'm sure you've met Jasmine in operations."

Jasmine was the computer whiz.

"Yes, of course."

"I trained her."

If there was any truth to Brenda/Traci's story, she was definitely a force to be reckoned with. Jasmine could do things with a computer that most geniuses never even dreamed of. So if Jasmine had been taught by the woman in front of Mia, then Brenda/Traci's skills were phenomenal.

"Now I am impressed. *If* what you're saying is true."

"You don't have to believe me. I know what I'm capable of and I'm pretty sure that once you and Jean have that little chat she will verify everything that I've said. Now back to Michael. He's running an elite escort service. He's raking in millions a year."

Mia felt a wave of nausea surge up to her throat.

"His list of clients could cripple the city if their names were ever exposed. It includes everyone from politicians to Fortune 500 executives and bank presidents, and not only here but out-of-state as well."

"How do you know this?"

"I know because I've been to the parties. I've seen the women. It's all very discreet, mind you. Unless you were really looking, you would never know. I didn't for a while. But then I started seeing some of the same women's faces with different men at different private events. I've never said a word to him about it. He has no idea that I know. But once I became suspicious, I tapped into his computer. I found the file."

It was probably the same file that she'd found, Mia thought.

Mia's door opened.

Brenda twisted in her seat. Before she could react, Bernard had a handkerchief over her mouth and she crumbled in her seat.

"I'll take it from here. Jean wants to see both of you within the hour."

He picked Brenda up, braced her against him and put his arm around her waist to keep her on her feet. "Hand me her coat and purse."

Mia numbly did as she was instructed.

He half dragged, half walked her out. Mia rushed to the front of the office and saw the black Ford Explorer parked at the curb. If she didn't know better, she'd swear that was Claudia, Savannah's mother, on the other side of the tinted windows behind the wheel.

Bernard settled Brenda into the backseat, got in beside her, and the SUV pulled off.

It was a scene right out of a James Bond movie.

Mia pressed her hand to her chest. She needed a drink.

"You want to bring me up to speed?" Ashley asked, snapping Mia out of her trance.

Mia blinked, bringing Ashley into focus. For a moment, Mia was disoriented—nothing made any sense. But in the next minute she was pissed. What the hell was going on? First Ashley was right under her nose and now Brenda. She suddenly didn't know what was real and what wasn't. And the in-her-mind relationship with Michael was a perfect example of how she was no longer able to separate fact from fiction.

She turned on Ashley. "Is Ashley even your real name?" she railed. "What other secrets do you have that I should know about? Are you really here to spy on me, make me crazy? What did Jean do to her to make her want to have a whole other life? My God, what have I gotten myself into?"

Burning tears of anger and frustration filled her eyes and spilled over her eyelids.

Ashley stepped toward her gingerly. She put her hands on Mia's stiff shoulders. "Mia, calm down. Okay? I know all this seems too much right now, but it's going to be all right. I promise."

Mia slapped her hands away. "Just leave me alone." She held up her hands. "Leave me alone!"

Ashley took a step back. "Fine. Let me know when you're ready to see Jean. I'll be out front."

Mia spun away. On wooden legs she went to the love seat in the corner and collapsed into it. She pressed her head against the back of the couch and wept. What she needed right at that moment were the strong arms of her man wrapped tightly around her, telling her that it was going to be all right. But if she knew nothing else, she knew that, at best, that little desire was hours from fruition.

They took Ashley's Infiniti for the drive uptown to Harlem. The first few minutes of the ride were done in silence. The only sounds were the intermittent street noises.

Finally, Mia spoke. "I'm sorry for going off on you earlier. There was no excuse for taking my frustration out on you." She turned halfway in her seat. "I apologize. Really."

"No problem. If anyone understands how this whole thing can get to you, I do. So forget the apology. Chalk it up to stress."

Mia faced forward. "Will you be honest with me?"

"Sure."

"Did you know Brenda or Traci?"

Ashley shook her head. "No. She was gone before I came along. I'd heard about one of the members leaving, but it was always very hush-hush. No one would talk about it."

"Hmm." She was thoughtful for a moment then frowned. "How come your picture isn't up on the hall of fame?"

Ashley laughed. "It is. It's not in the main corridor to Jean's office. It's on the top floor. Most newbies don't have access. In addition to which, when Jean assigned me to you, she intentionally moved it. Even if you had seen it you probably wouldn't have recognized me without my Angela Davis fro." She patted her halo of naturally spiral curls.

Mia chuckled. "I can't imagine you without it."

"There was a time," she singsonged.

"What about Brenda?"

"As I said, I'd never met her before. My guess is that once she'd left the agency—and not under the best of circumstances and with Jean literally erasing her out of existence—Jean would have taken the picture down."

"You're probably right. Does Jean scare you?"

"Scare me? What do you mean?"

"It's like sometimes she doesn't have a soul and everyone is expendable in her life. It's all about the job, at any cost."

"For her, it is. She's really not as coldhearted as you think. Jean…Jean has had a real rough time of it in relationships and in the career path that she chose. She was screwed over in the CIA by people less qualified than her and badly hurt by her husband."

"Husband? I didn't know she was married."

"She isn't now, but she was. What happened between them changed her a lot. She only refers to him as Mr. Armstrong. Look, I really shouldn't be telling you this. Maybe one day she'll tell you all about it. Maybe she won't. All I can say is that beneath that cold, hard-ass exterior is a real decent human being. Even if she does act like a machine," she tossed in with a smile.

"I'll try to keep that in mind."

"Let me put it this way. She changed my life when it desperately needed changing, and I will always be grateful to her for that."

"Changed your life? How?"

She turned her head to look at Mia. "I was at the bottom of the food chain, strung out, living on the street…she rescued me, gave me a life. But that's another story for another day."

Mia rested back against the leather seat. The last person on earth she thought had a caring bone in her body was Jean Wallington-Armstrong. This little bit of information forced her to look at Jean from a different perspective. There's always more to a person than meets the eye. No truer adage had even been written, especially when it came to the Ladies Cartel.

They pulled up in front of the brownstone.

Showtime.

Chapter 17

Claudia met Ashley and Mia at the front door when they rang the bell. Her expression was somber. "Jean is upstairs."

Mia and Ashley walked inside behind Claudia.

"Where's Brenda or Traci whatever her name is?" Mia asked.

"She's here. Jean will explain everything," Claudia replied.

After Mia and Ashley were seated, Jean didn't waste any time getting to the point.

"I'm sure you are both aware that there has been a serious breach in security." Her gaze darted in Brenda/Traci's direction, who only sat up straighter in her seat, as if challenging Jean in her own way.

"So that we are all on the same page," she began again. "Brenda Forde, known to me as Traci Bennett, was a former member of the Cartel who was decommissioned of her own accord five years ago. To my knowledge—" she cleared her throat "—Traci was off the radar and living her life, apparently much closer than I ever realized. For reasons that she has explained to me, she is willing to help us get as much inside information as necessary in the Avante Enterprises case. I'm sure that the both of you understand that because of the way she approached you we had no recourse but to take her in as quickly and as quietly as possible for questioning.

"To reassure you both, we are running a thorough check on her, using all our resources to guarantee that she will not be in a position to compromise us in any way. When the report is back, which I suspect will be shortly, I will give the clearance so that we can proceed as planned and whatever help Traci can offer will be accepted at that point."

"How can you be sure that this isn't some kind of setup to infiltrate the Cartel?" Ashley asked.

"I can't. At least not right now, which is why she was drugged and blindfolded before she was brought here." She stole another look at Traci. "She has no idea where she is."

Mia was certain this was some weird out-of-body experience. The whole scene was surreal. Right down to the characters, the dimly lit room and the manipulating head of operations moving people around like a grand puppeteer. At that moment, she wanted to jump up and run the hell out as fast and as far as she could. She wanted to have the nerve that Traci did and get out before she got dragged down so far that there was no way out. But who was to say that she wouldn't wind up just like Traci, right back in the place she was trying to get away from?

A knock on the door drew everyone's attention. Jasmine stepped inside. She spotted Traci sitting off to the side and there was the flash of recognition, followed by a look of admiration that quickly passed. "I have that report." She handed over a manila folder to Jean. "I sifted through all the intel and took out the extraneous information. Only the relevant data is included."

Jean snapped her gaze up from the papers in front of her. "The next time that I ask you to compile data on a potential rogue I want all the data! Not only what you think is important. *I* make those decisions. Understood?"

The entire room froze in shocked disbelief. Jean never lost her cool, and certainly never lost her temper. But it was clear that this mini-explosion was an indication that she was rattled.

Jasmine visibly recoiled from the verbal assault. "Yes. Of course. I'll recompile the data." She turned to leave, keeping her gaze focused on her Reeboks.

"Jasmine."

She stopped with her hand on the knob and turned halfway. "Yes?"

Jean lifted her chin ever so slightly. "That won't be necessary," she said in what must be her apologetic tone. "I'm sure this will be sufficient. I can look at everything at a later time. If I think I need more, I'll let you know."

Jasmine only nodded and walked out, closing the door quietly behind her.

Jean took a seat behind her desk, slipped on her red-framed glasses, flipped open the folder and began to read. You could hear a pin drop in the room, the rhythm of heartbeats, the turn of a page. For a solid fifteen minutes, no one dared to move or breathe out loud. Finally she closed the folder, removed her glasses and turned to Traci. "It appears that everything you've said regarding your whereabouts, your activities since leaving the Cartel checks out."

Traci's features, which had remained taut throughout this ordeal, slowly began to relax. She gave Jean a barely there nod of her head.

"Although Traci will not be given full access to or privileges of the Cartel, she says that she is willing to help us bring down Avante Enterprises and Michael Burke. As you know, Avante is a front for an illegal escort service. We have names and amounts, but what we don't have is irrefutable proof. We don't have transactions taking place, photographs, audio or locations. This is where Traci can be of assistance."

"I know Michael," Traci began, "and, more importantly, I know how the legitimate end of the business works. I have access to the files, the computers and all the people Michael knows and associates with." She zeroed in on Mia. "The red-carpet event that you're running on Friday for Raven…I know that many of the women will be there. I can point them out."

"I'd like to bring in Danielle," Mia said.

"Explain," Jean said curtly.

"We can use the extra hands, especially when it comes to perhaps photographing the attendees, overhearing conversations."

Jean was thoughtful for a moment. "Fine, bring her in." Jean exhaled. She looked from one to the other. "Anything else that you can think of?"

"No."

"We'll talk again the morning of the red carpet to ensure that everyone is in place and you have what you need, Mia."

Mia nodded.

Ashley stood up and Mia followed suit. They took one last look at Traci and walked out. Bernard was right behind them.

"I still don't know if I can trust you," Jean said, once they were alone. She turned to face Traci. "You left once before, nearly ruining a case as a result. How do I know that you won't suddenly have a change of heart for this man you claim to have fallen for and just tell him everything?"

"I wouldn't do anything to risk exposing the Cartel or an operation. You know that."

"It seems that lately I don't know much of anything anymore. I thought I did." Her tone sounded uncharacteristically weak, sad almost, as if for the very first time she was faced with the knowledge of her own vulnerability. "But until I can be sure about you and your real motives, I want you to stay in the background and if you can't, I'm sure you know that I can make that happen."

"There's no reason to threaten me, Jean. I'm not here to hurt you or the organization. I want to see Michael brought down."

"Because you're a woman scorned or because you really believe what he's doing is wrong?" she taunted.

Traci's jaw clenched. "Maybe a little of both."

"But why come back now?"

She glanced away. "I've known that Michael didn't love me, but I thought he at least cared for and respected me. When I stumbled across those files, everything that I thought about him began to crumble. I didn't want to believe it. I wanted to be wrong. And then Mia shows up and I can see in an instant where his heart is and has always been. I guess something inside me snapped and when I found the listening device and knew the source, whatever kind of fleeting hope or desire I may have had regarding me and Michael vanished. I realized that what I'd found had merit and it wasn't my imagination because the Cartel was already investigating him."

"You disappointed me, Traci," she said, her voice leaden with regret. "You were the best. You were more than a Cartel member, you were like my own child." She turned sad eyes on Traci, eyes begging to understand what she'd done that had prompted Traci to run away.

"I guess I can tell you now."

"Tell me what now?"

"The truth about why I really left the Cartel when I was in Chicago. I can finally tell you about that scumbag you married," she said, her voice hard with emotion.

"What! What the hell are you talking about?"

"Your husband tried to sleep with me. Not once, not twice, but every chance he got, which was many, since I was always at your home."

Jean's face blanched. "W-what are you saying?"

"Yes, Eric Armstrong. He went so far as to blackmail me into sleeping with him."

Jean flinched. "Why are you lying? He wouldn't do that!"

"Of course he would. Eric was as manipulative as you are. It's why you both got along up to a point. But Eric was manipulative for his own greedy reasons." She crossed the room then walked back, talking as she did. "To this day I don't know how he did it. He had an audiotape of my voice—calling him, telling him…things. Talking about how great it was between us, what I wanted him to do to me the next time we were together." She rubbed her hands up and down her arms as if she'd suddenly gotten a chill. She stopped walking and turned to look straight at Jean. "He told me that he was going to give you the tapes if I didn't sleep with him. I couldn't let him do that." She shook her head, her gaze looking back to that ugly time in her past. "You were so in love with him. Happy for the first time since I'd known you. I mean, really happy. I knew if he gave those to you, it would kill you inside, ruin our relationship. I couldn't let him do it. So I left. I left the Cartel and my whole life so that I wouldn't ruin yours."

Jean's face was so pale it became translucent. She didn't move. She didn't speak. Slowly she lowered herself into her chair. With what appeared to be almost painful understanding, she leveled her gaze on Traci.

"Giving you this information and helping is my way of making up for walking out on you and not telling you what kind of bastard you were married to." She pressed her fist to her mouth then moved it away, drawing in air through her mouth. "When I found out what Michael was doing, it brought it all back—women being used—even if they are getting paid."

"I...think I always knew," Jean said, her words barely above a whisper. "I knew he saw other women, but I turned a blind eye because I loved him." Her throat worked up and down. She blinked several times. "But never this. Not what he tried to do to you. I'm so sorry, Traci." She slowly shook her head, her eyes pleading for forgiveness.

They moved simultaneously toward each other and embraced, erasing all the years that had separated them.

Chapter 18

Mia and Ashley left Bernard at the brownstone and started back to the office.

"So what do you make of everything that happened back there?" Mia asked as they pulled out into the late-afternoon Manhattan traffic.

"I think the thing that freaks me out the most is to realize that Jean is not infallible. That she really doesn't know everything and that there was actually someone out there who had outsmarted her—for years. That scares me because Jean scares me. But Traci is the real deal."

Mia nodded in agreement. "I know exactly what you mean. Not to see Jean in total control was a reality check, to say the least."

"So it looks like we're going to be working with Traci. How do you feel about that?"

"You mean because of her relationship with Michael?"

"Yeah."

"Hmm. I don't feel anything one way or the other. Whatever illusions I may have had about Michael have been crushed. To be truthful, I feel bad for Traci. Michael is a charismatic man. His aura can overwhelm you and before you know it you're totally mesmerized by him, doing things you never would have thought you would do. And when your heart and emotions are all tied up in it, it's that much more devastating. But from what I've seen so far, Traci is a strong woman. She'll be fine."

"Damn, I was looking forward to the catfight!"

Mia poked her in the arm and they both laughed.

"We still need to figure out what we're going to do with my Michelle connection," Ashley was saying as they left the car and walked into the office.

"That's where I think Danielle can play a role."

"How?"

Mia opened her office door; the soft winter white and creams instantly soothed her. Ashley came behind her.

"I'm thinking that since you obviously cannot be at the event on Friday, in case Michelle is there and recognizes you, Danielle could be a potential candidate."

Ashley frowned. "Color me slow. I'm not getting you."

Mia grinned. "Sorry, it's in my head and not making it out of my mouth." She leaned against the edge of desk and folded her arms. "I want you to contact Michelle. Tell her that you have a friend who would be interested in her offer. You want to bring her by the bar to meet her and see what she thinks. That someone is going to be Danielle. We need her on-site on Friday, and that will be the perfect way to do it. Michael has never met her. There would be no reason for him to suspect anything."

A slow smile of understanding moved across Ashley's mouth. "Gotcha."

"I'll call Danielle and bring her up to speed. You get in touch with Michelle."

"I'm on it." Ashley walked out and went up front.

Mia went behind her desk and sat down. Maybe this whole mess would come together after all. She dug in her bag and pulled out her cell. The glitches and surprises were seriously attacking her orderly state of mind. She dialed Danielle.

"Hey, Dani, got a minute?"

"Just barely. I'm in the middle of a photo shoot. What's up?"

"I'm going to need your help to pull this assignment off."

"What do you need me to do? Something exciting, I hope."

Mia chuckled. "Let's just say you'll have to get dressed up and be fabulous."

"Right up my alley. Sounds easy."

"Well, it's a bit more complicated than that. I'm going to need you to be available to go with Ashley to meet Michelle at the bar. You're going to apply for one of the 'extra income' positions."

"Ohh," she said, understanding dawning. "When?"

"Ashley is trying to contact Michelle now. As soon as she can set up a time, I'll let you know. Obviously, it needs to be sooner rather than later."

"No problem. I'll work it out. Look, I gotta run. Call me."

"Thanks, sis."

"Of course. Later."

With that done, she pulled out her PDA, connected it to her computer and put on her headset. She set her computer and PDA to the communications program that was continuously recording Michael's phone calls at his office and home in Sag Harbor. Although she had access to both locations at any given time, the past few days and the information that she'd uncovered had been more than she had been prepared to handle. Hearing anything more incriminating moved down on her agenda. However, she was supposed to report her findings to Jean and the last thing she wanted Jean to think was that she was slacking off in her role because of residual feelings that she may still have for Michael.

The radio frequency grid came up on her screen in two panels—one attached to his office, the other to his home. At the moment, both were flat, meaning that he wasn't on either phone. She clicked on the Archives link to recover anything recorded in the past five days when she noticed the flat green iridescent line in the second panel on her computer screen. He was on his office phone. She adjusted her headset and pushed up the volume.

"It's Mike. I need to make some transfers from here to the Caymans."

"When?"

"Today. You have all the information."

"Today?"

"I think this game has run its course. I want to protect what I've gained so far. Then I'm getting out."

"Don't tell me anything you don't want me to know. That's our agreement."

"Fine. Just get it done, Andy. Okay. Call me when you have it taken care of."

"Do you want everything moved?"

"Everything."

"I'll call you tonight with the confirmation numbers."

"Thanks."

The call disconnected.

Slowly, Mia removed the headphones and set them down on the desk. She frowned in concentration. What was he doing? Of course, if he was talking about the Caymans, she knew it had to be a money transfer. He'd also mentioned getting out. Was he getting out of the escort business, taking the money and running?

Then that voice that was in the back of her head started talking to her. The voice that kept telling her that she still had feelings for Michael. The voice that would whisper to her and tell her that this was all some ugly mistake.

If he was given enough time and space, maybe he could get away before the law came swooping down on him. It was still hard for her to imagine that when this was all over, Michael would go to jail and she would be responsible for putting him there. It was a weight of guilt that she, deep down in her soul, didn't want to carry. Maybe if he just had some time, the voice whispered. No one has to know, it urged.

Mia jumped up from her seat, banishing the urgent whispers from her head. She needed to ground herself, clear those traitorous thoughts from her head. She reached for the phone on her desk and dialed Steven.

After being told that he was out of the office for the rest of the day, she felt bereft, and she knew herself. When she got in this unattached, disorganized space in her head, she began making mistakes and getting tense.

She drew in long, slow, deep breaths from her diaphragm and exhaled through her nose, as her tai chi instructor had told her years ago, when she'd taken up the relaxation art. It helped to soothe her, as it did now. After about ten minutes, she could feel her jangled nerves evening out, the racing of her heart beginning to slow and her thoughts starting to line back up. She opened her eyes. Everything was going to be fine. She was going to make this work. She checked her computer again to make sure that she'd saved the file she'd just listened to, then downloaded all the recordings to date on a flash drive ready to hand over to Jean at their next meeting.

With Cartel business out of the way, she turned her attention to running her business.

"Hey, Michelle, it's Ashley. Remember me?"

"Of course. How are you? Did you make that call like I told you?"

"Actually, no. And only because I know I'm going to be out of town for a while. But that's not the reason I called. I got the impression that you sort of have an in with that guy Michael. Well, I want to give a very good friend of mine an opportunity. She could definitely use the extra money. She's gorgeous and would look good on any man's arm. I was hoping that you might have some time to meet her, see what you think."

Michelle was silent for a moment. "How close is this friend to you? I mean, this is not something that you tell everyone you know. If you can't be discreet… Look, forget we ever had a conversation. This isn't cool."

"Wait, listen. This woman is cool. I've known her since high school. I didn't give her any details, other than she may have a chance to make some extra money just for looking good for a few hours. She was all for it. But that's all she knows. You meet her, feel her out. If it seems good to you, then make a decision then." Ashley held her breath. She couldn't blow this now.

"Can you be here at the club around seven tonight?"

"Not a problem."

"Okay. And listen. No more recruits. That's my job."

Ashley's brow rose. "See you at seven." She hung up the phone and breathed a sigh of relief, just as Mia approached.

"Did you make contact?"

"Just got off the phone with her." She explained what had happened and how they had almost lost that connection.

"Good thinking on your part," Mia said. "We definitely can't let her get suspicious or say anything to Michael."

"Exactly. Guess you should give Danielle a call and let her know about tonight. We need to figure out where to meet up."

"Here's her cell number. I spoke with her a while ago and gave her a heads-up. She's actually on location right now. Leave a message on her voice mail. Makes more sense for you to call with particulars than me."

"True." She took the number. "I'll call her in a little."

"Okay. I'm going to run over to check on the venue for tomorrow night. When I get back, we'll go over the final punch list. If you can touch base with the videographer and the lighting people to let them know we want to do a run-through tomorrow at 10:00 a.m., that would be great."

"I'm on it."

Mia returned to her office, grabbed her bag and tote then headed out.

Ashley had arranged to meet Danielle on Chelsea Piers at six-thirty to go over the strategy. They were best friends since high school. They both attended Boys & Girls High School in Bedford-Stuyvesant in Brooklyn, and now both of them worked for Mia's firm. Neither of them were married or currently involved. And they needed the extra income to get out of debt and breathe a little easier.

Once their stories were in sync, they headed over to the Last Call Bar & Grill.

As usual, Danielle was totally the fashion diva. Her naturally wavy hair fell in soft cascades around her face, over her shoulders and halfway down her back. She was a solid size 10, full and curvy, and she kept her body encased in only the best. Today she wore an M. Preston two-piece pantsuit in crimson, with bold bulky silver jewelry at her throat and wrist. A silky white camisole peeked out from the top of the jacket. And to complete the ensemble, she wore a pair of black alligator ankle boots.

When Ashley saw her, she was amazed at how stunning Danielle was. Of course, she'd seen her on several occasions at the TLC headquarters and was always impressed with her natural beauty. But she'd never really seen Danielle put it all together as she did now. No way could Michelle not be impressed.

"Do you go to work dressed like that?" Ashley asked as they approached the bar.

Danielle took off her dark shades as they stepped into the dim interior. "No, I ran home and changed. Didn't think I'd make a good impression with my sweaty T-shirt and jeans."

"There she is," Ashley said under her breath. "The one with the pink tank top."

They approached and took seats next to each other at the end of the bar. They had that end to themselves. Several moments passed before Michelle came over.

"How are you ladies doing this evening? What can I get you?"

"I'll take a coke with lemon," Ashley said.

"Same for me."

Michelle looked at Danielle for a long moment. "Be right back."

"I think she's trying to play it real cool," Ashley said. "When we met for the first time, she was Ms. Chatty Cathy."

Michelle returned with their sodas. "My boss is working the bar tonight," she said in a pseudo-whisper. "He'll be here for another hour. Can't really talk until then."

"No problem. We can wait," Ashley said. "What do you have on the menu?"

Michelle handed them a menu and they ordered a plate of buffalo wings with blue cheese and celery sticks.

"Coming right up. You can have a seat at one of the tables if you like. Or you can eat at the bar. Your choice."

Danielle turned to Ashley. "Table sounds good."

They took their drinks, got up and headed to an open table.

"Looks like it's going to be a long night."

Ashley pursed her lips as they sat down. "Unfortunately. But it will give us a chance to get to know each other. How did you get involved in the Cartel?"

"Through Savannah. I guess you probably know that her

mom, Claudia, recruited her." She laughed lightly. "Well, Mia and I actually helped Savannah out on her first assignment. When she got her next assignment, she couldn't take it on, the pregnancy was kicking her butt. Oh, you have got to meet her baby girl, Mikayla. She will steal your heart and then the show." She smiled, thinking of her. "We're all her godmothers. Anyway, when Savannah couldn't take on the job, she asked Mia and me. Well, Mia was going to be out of town so I got the job. Almost blew it, but it all worked out."

"It usually does."

"Can I get you ladies anything to drink?" a waitress asked.

"No. I'm good," Ashley said, holding up her glass of soda.

"Me, too, thanks."

"Your order should be ready shortly."

"What about you? I mean, I thought I knew you, but obviously I didn't. Do you have anyone special in your life?" Danielle asked.

"No. Not at the moment. A long moment," Ashley added with a short laugh. "But I'm always hopeful. I'm sure there's someone out there who would be interested in a quirky, blues-loving, former homeless woman turned secret agent. I mean, after all, this is New York."

"You have a lot going for you. You'll find the right man at the right time. I never thought I'd actually settle down with one man until I met Nick. It was a struggle at first, but we worked through it. Both of us came into the relationship with a lot of emotional baggage. But the load is much lighter now."

The waitress appeared with their platter of buffalo wings and they dug in. They spent the next hour talking about everything from the upcoming presidential election to women's rights and the sagging pants on young boys. The more they talked, the more they realized all the things they had in common.

Danielle really liked Ashley and could see why Mia liked her so much.

They were engaged in a hot debate about Star Jones's miraculous weight loss when Michelle came up to their table. She took a seat next to Ashley.

"Sorry. Never can tell when the boss is going to show up." She looked around. The club was relatively empty. "I guess it's okay to talk here." She focused her attention on Danielle. "So your friend tells me that you're interested in making some extra money."

"Yes, I am. She also told me that you're the one who can make that happen."

The corner of Michelle's wide mouth quirked upward. "Something like that. But the final decision is not up to me. I can only make recommendations. So why don't you tell me something about yourself."

Danielle gave her the spiel that she and Ashley had gone over.

Michelle nodded as Danielle spoke. She looked at Ashley once Danielle was finished speaking. "I think she might be okay. I like her." She leaned forward. "There's a major party coming up Friday night. Some blowout red-carpet event. I'll introduce you to Michael then. Are you available?"

Danielle casually flipped her hand. "Sounds perfect. I'll make myself available."

"That's what I like to hear." She wrote down the address for the party on a napkin, then pushed up from the table. "See you on Friday."

Ashley and Danielle walked toward their car.

"Looks like we're in," Ashley said, opening the door.

"Yes, indeedy."

Chapter 19

The stretch limos, luxury sedans and chauffeur-driven SUVs lined up along Park Avenue as one after another of the icons of the music industry, accompanied by their entourage, strutted onto the red carpet and into the grand foyer of the hotel.

Flashbulbs popped in rapid succession as every news outlet vied for the money shots of the glitterati who sparkled in the night like the diamonds that adorned their wrists, necks, ears and fingers.

Every time a new car pulled up in front of the venue, the media went wild, hoping to get a shot of the elusive Raven.

Reps from TMZ, BET J, Page Six, *Entertainment Tonight, Access Hollywood,* photographers from all the hip-hop magazines, and A&R execs from the major labels were in attendance, from Arista to J Records, Atlantic to Bad Boy and everything in between.

The dons and divas of hip-hop were also in attendance: Jigga and his new bride, Usher, Mary, Diddy, Alicia, John and even old-school royalty made their presence felt with Eddie Lavert, Pattie and Gladys.

The walls had been covered in voluminous sheer draping with silver thread running through them. Lighting came from behind the draping, giving the impression that the event was floating on clouds. Waiters and waitresses in white and silver worked the crowd with trays of appetizers that included stuffed clams, grilled shrimp, caviar, an assortment of cheeses and sushi. Huge jumbo monitors hung from the ceiling, displaying videos of Raven in concert, rare interviews and other footage. An eight-piece band played underneath the rumble of soft and deep voices and squeals of delight.

Mia was so thrilled with the turnout and the presentation of the venue space that she was almost nervous. She checked and rechecked every element of the evening so many times that the staff began to give her dirty looks.

Savannah took her by the arm the tenth time she flew by.

"Mia, you have got to relax, girl. You're going to break a vessel or something. Everything is perfect." She squeezed her hand. "Seriously. And if you took a breath, you'd realize it yourself."

"Oh, am I really that bad? I'm just doing my job. My company's reputation is on the line. Not to mention—" she lowered her voice "—the other thing we have going on. Have you seen Danielle yet?"

"No. But as we planned, she will be coming with Michelle."

Mia drew in a breath. "Right. Right." She squinted around the room. There had to be more than two hundred guests. She'd hired some temps to help with the check-in, and security was tighter than the Pentagon.

"Fabulous job," a woman singsonged as she passed Mia and Savannah.

"See? Told you."

Mia chuckled. "Okay, okay. Blake has the baby?"

"Yep. It's a father-daughter night. I told him to give Steve a call to come and keep him company. So they will be occupied for the evening."

"Thanks, sweetie. Oh, there are Michelle and Danielle."

"Gotta act like we don't know them."

Danielle caught Savannah's and Mia's eyes and casually indicated the square-shaped catch on her purse by tapping it as they moved through the crowd into the main ballroom.

Mia nodded in acknowledgment. She turned to Savannah. "Let me go mingle and make sure everything is running smoothly. Traci is hand-holding Michael, and Ashley insisted on being part of the operation. She's out there on the street somewhere, posing as media."

"That'll work. We're going to need all the photos we can get. Is she going to be able to come inside?"

"I thought it was too risky. On the off chance that Michelle might recognize her—or Michael, for that matter. But she said she could pull it off. And with a crowd this size, it should be fine. But keep your eyes and ears open. I'll check back with you later." She headed over to Brenda/Traci and Michael.

"Hi. So what do you think so far?" Mia asked, her eyes flitting around the room as she tried to keep it all in focus. She wished she could put her glasses on, but vanity prevailed.

"Looks like you've outdone yourself, Mia," Michael said. "The spread is fantastic. The band is great and the entire décor is spectacular."

"I couldn't agree more. I've been eavesdropping on some of the guests and everyone is blown away." Mia pressed her hands together at the center of her chest. "After the first hour, we'll move inside and the entertainment will begin."

Michael nodded. He turned to Traci. "Brenda, will you excuse us for a minute?"

"Sure, I'm going to mingle."

When Traci was out of earshot, he turned to Mia. "I knew I'd made the right decision when I asked you to take on this project." He stepped a little closer. "You look beautiful tonight." He ran his hand across her bare shoulder.

She fought not to flinch at his touch, beating back the memories. "Thank you. We worked hard."

"Where is Ashley, by the way? I didn't see her around."

"She was here earlier getting everything set up."

He nodded. "Maybe you and I can get together after the event."

"I don't think so. It's going to be a long night."

"We need to talk."

"About what?"

"Us."

"Michael—"

He held up his hand. "Not now. But we will. There's so much I want to tell you."

The look of warmth and sincerity in his eyes set her stomach fluttering. She glanced away. She couldn't be dragged back into the abyss of charisma again.

She looked at her watch. "I need to make the rounds."

He nodded as she walked away.

"Michael!"

He turned toward the sound of his name being called. Michelle was walking toward him with a woman so stunning it took away his breath for a moment. This must be the woman Michelle had spoken to him about, he thought. At least he hoped so. She would be perfect.

"Michael, this is Danielle Holloway. Danielle, Michael Burke, CEO of Avante Enterprises and the driving force behind this event."

Michael shrugged off the accolades and zeroed in on Danielle. He extended his hand. "Ms. Holloway, a pleasure to meet you."

"Thank you. I've heard great things about you from Michelle."

"Michelle is better than paid advertising." He paused, looked Danielle over, taking in her champagne-colored sheath gown, which dipped to a delicious low in the front and a dangerous plunge in the back. The silky fabric glided over her curves, the color so perfectly matched to her skin tone that upon first glance it gave her the illusion of being a naked Venus. Her dark mane of hair was piled on top of her head, reminiscent of the goddesses of Greek mythology.

"So what do you do, Danielle?"

"I'm a freelance writer," she said.

"Really. I'm sure you could find plenty to write about tonight."

She cocked a brow. "True. But, unfortunately, assignments like these usually go to the regulars. We freelancers may get the leftovers, or if someone bows out. It's a tough life."

"I can imagine." He placed his hand on her arm. "Let's talk." They walked over to a semi-quiet corner near the bar. "Can I get you a drink?"

"No, thank you. I'm fine." She pressed the button on the catch on her purse.

"So, Michelle tells me you're looking to make some extra money."

"Yes, I am. And she also said you were the one to make that happen." She looked up at him from beneath smoky lashes.

Michael grinned.

"So, tell me, what is it that I would be doing?"

"I have associates, very important associates, who some-times…need attention. They may be in town, unfamiliar with how to get around, or simply want a beautiful woman to accompany them to an event."

"I see. Sounds simple enough. How do I make money doing that?"

"Depending on the event, the amount of hours of your time will determine your fee. Every now and then a gentleman may want you to accompany him to one of the Caribbean islands. That ups your fee, of course. And they are responsible for all expenses."

Danielle nodded and hoped that the recording device was catching every word.

"So how does that sound?"

"I'm interested, if that's what you want to know. My time is my own—no ties." She shrugged sexily.

"I was hoping that's what you would say. Let me introduce you to some of my associates. People you will certainly get to know much better. Then I'll have Michelle introduce you to some of the ladies."

Traci and Mia walked through the crowd.

"See the woman in the black Vera Wang near the caviar?" Traci asked.

Mia squinted until the woman came into focus. "Yes."

"She's a regular. She's at every event and usually goes off with one of the guests by night's end." She jutted her chin in the direction of a couple talking over glasses of champagne. "That's the CEO of Bankers Union, one of the largest bank conglomerates in the country. The woman next to him is Dina. She's been on the payroll for a while."

As Traci scoped the room, she pointed out nearly a dozen classy, highly attractive women who were on Michael's list of eligible escorts.

"Do you have any idea where they all live? Are they from New York?"

"That I don't know," Traci admitted.

"Ms. Turner."

Mia turned behind her. "Yes?"

"Hi, I'm a reporter from *The Times* Entertainment Section. I was hoping to steal a few minutes of your time."

"Me?"

"Yes, you were responsible for putting this together, correct?"

"I am. Yes."

"I wanted to ask you about your business, how you built it, got to this point. Things like that. A short profile. It will only take a few minutes. Promise. I know how busy you must be."

"I can give you about five minutes. I need to get ready for the entertainment portion of the evening."

"I'll catch up with you later," Traci said, then walked off to talk with a group that included one of the A&R execs from Atlantic.

"Jean sent me," the woman said, as soon as they were alone.

Mia's open expression froze. "Excuse me?"

"Jean sent me. She said to be sure that you don't try to take Michael down tonight. You are only to gather whatever information you can. It's too open and there's too much media. And she doesn't want your name and business tied into this at all. She wants everyone involved to meet at the brownstone tomorrow morning at ten."

Before Mia could respond, the woman walked away and out. For several moments she didn't move. Suddenly she was chilled, and rubbed her hands up and down her bare arms.

"I'm sure I can find a way to warm you up," a deep voice whispered from behind her.

Her heart thudded. She turned around. "Michael."

He kissed her cheek. "I've been hearing nothing but good things all evening. Congratulations."

"Thanks." She was still rattled by the visit from one of Jean's operatives.

Michael frowned. "Is everything okay?"

She swallowed. "Yes. I'll settle down once the night is finally over."

He rubbed her arm. "I've never known you to be nervous," he said, looking at her curiously.

"Just a very hectic night." Her eyes darted around the space. "I need to get ready for the entertainment, check with the sound men and the video." She checked her watch. "Raven should be here in about an hour."

Michael nodded.

"She's going to show up, right?"

"That's what her people promised me."

It was the only piece of the puzzle that she couldn't guarantee.

"I've really got to go." She started to move away.

Michael clasped her wrist. "Wait. I want to talk to you…about another event. A lot less people, more intimate, at my place in the Poconos. I want to put something together for some close friends."

She was ready to turn it down, but Jean's directive stuck in her head. This might be another opportunity to get more information. "Can we talk tomorrow?"

"Over lunch." It wasn't a question.

She hesitated. "Fine." She hurried away.

Raven's performance went off without a hitch, just the way it was planned. The crowd loved her. The media was frantic that they didn't get a chance to interview her. But her mystique stayed intact and Mia had a friend for life.

Tomorrow was another day and another meeting with Jean.

Chapter 20

With all the ladies having other lives, they'd agreed before leaving the party the night before to meet at the brownstone by eight. Hopefully, it wouldn't take too long and they could return to their livelihoods.

Mia, Savannah, Traci, Danielle and Ashley all arrived within minutes of each other and gathered together in the main room on the ground floor.

It had turned decidedly chilly overnight and the warmth of the brownstone was a welcome relief. They'd all dressed for the weather, sporting everything from lined leather jackets to jazzy cashmere car coats. Mia, always one to show off her long legs, wore a short ink-black wool skirt and black leather pumps topped with a winter-white silk sweater and a fire-engine red shawl, draped dramatically around her neck and shoulders. Savannah, relishing the fact that she could finally fit into her clothes after the baby, was fashion-ready in a two-piece, camel-colored suit with bold bronze-colored buttons and three-inch Jimmy Choo chocolate-brown heels. Ashley, always elegantly casual, wore gray suede pants with an over-size black cowl-neck sweater, accessorized with silver at her wrists and dangling from her earlobes. Danielle, who always looked as if she'd just stepped off the cover of a magazine, wore denim as only Danielle could, the short battle jacket and matching jeans accented with chunky jewelry and her sig-nature ankle boots. Not to be outdone, Traci was corporate sharp in a hunter-green, two-piece skirt suit, cinched at the waist to subtly accentuate her hips.

To a casual observer it looked like a gathering of heads of the fashion or entertainment industry.

Jean had set out a continental breakfast, anticipating their early arrival and need for expediency.

As they sat around sipping herbal tea and imported coffee, and munching on croissants and muffins, Jean came in, fol-lowed by Jasmine.

"Good morning, ladies. I know we don't have much time so this will be as brief as possible. Mia has sent over all the footage from last night and Danielle provided the recorded conversation she had with Michael Burke. At first blush, it appeared that we had enough to go on. But after reviewing the audiotape and running it past the attorney general, there is not enough on there to bring an indictment. A good lawyer would tear what we have apart. We need concrete evidence."

Low groans bounced around the room.

"That is not anyone's fault. There wasn't anything that could have been done better," she said, directing her comment to Danielle. "The most important thing was that we couldn't appear to be entrapping anyone. Then all of your hard work would have been for nothing." She paused and looked around the room. "We're going to have to get more to nail him."

"We might have that chance," Mia offered. "He wants me to put together a private party for some close friends."

Jean nodded. "I see."

"I'm sure those private friends will be some of the men who were there last night," Traci said. "And I can guarantee that the women will be there as well."

"When is this party?" Jean asked.

"I'm not sure. I'm supposed to meet him for lunch to discuss what he wants and when."

Jean looked from one to the other. "My instincts tell me that this may be our last chance."

They all nodded.

"As soon as you have the details, I want to be informed, and a plan will be put in place." She paused. "Each of you has done a wonderful job. Simply because we didn't get all we needed last night does not mean that any of you did less than what you were supposed to do. We'll get him. I know you all have to get to your jobs, so I won't hold you any longer. Before we leave, is there anything you want to discuss, any questions?"

"What will happen if we can't get him to incriminate himself this next time?" Mia asked.

"We'll deal with that when the time comes. We're going to operate on the premise that he will incriminate himself and we will shut the operation down."

Nods of agreement all around.

"Ladies, have a great day." Jean walked out.

"I've got to run. Richard has a ten-o'clock court case this morning and if I'm not there to hold his hand, no telling what will happen to his poor client," Savannah joked.

Savannah worked as a paralegal for a private law firm with a great but needy boss. Danielle and Mia had been hounding her for years to go back to school and finish her law degree. Then she could hire Richard, since she was smarter than he was anyway and pretty much ran the company.

"Me, too," Traci said. "I'm going to work on getting an

advance copy of the guest list for the Poconos. If I do, I'll pass it along." She finished off her cup of tea, grabbed a blueberry muffin and headed out.

Jasmine caught up with her in the hallway.

"Traci…"

She stopped and turned.

Jasmine walked up to her. "It's good to have you back," she said quietly.

Traci smiled. "It's good to sort of be back. I'm just helping out."

"I didn't think I'd ever see you again…after everything went down with you and Jean."

Traci lowered her head. "It was a rough time. I didn't really have much of a choice. I had to leave, start over."

"So…are you part of the team again?" she asked, a hopeful hitch in her voice.

"We'll see. That's up to Jean."

"We could sure use you around here. We've had a few members from this region retire or move away."

Traci's chestnut-colored eyes, crinkled at the corners as she grinned. "How's the pay these days?"

"The per-assignment fee is still the same, but we get incentive bonuses, which is new."

"Hmm. Something to think about. Once this assignment is over I'll be out of a job. And again, it's not really up to me about coming back. It's up to Jean." She looked at her watch. "Oh, wow, I've got to run." She stepped up and embraced Jasmine, so very proud of her protégé.

"Even if you don't come back to TLC, let's not lose touch again," Jasmine spoke into Traci's ear.

Traci stepped back and held her shoulders. "We won't. I promise."

Jasmine tightened her lips and nodded as Traci hurried down the stairs and out into the street.

* * *

Traci arrived at Avante Enterprises and assumed her role as Brenda Forde, executive assistant. She checked in with the front desk for messages, then went to the office of the entertainment director to see if they'd downloaded any of the news articles on the red-carpet event for Raven. There were separate departments for entertainment, corporate and small business management, each headed by a different director with a two- or three-person staff. All the directors reported to her, and she, in turn, reported to Michael.

She took the printouts of the news clippings and went to her office. She took off her kidskin suede jacket and hung it on the standing rack in the corner of her office. Just as she sat down behind her smoked-glass desk, her phone rang. Peeking at the flashing light, she saw that it was Michael.

Bracing herself, she picked up.

"Yes. Good morning."

"Great event last night," he began.

"It certainly was."

"I was hoping you had a few minutes this morning before things got busy. I wanted to go over a couple of things with you."

She sighed to herself. "Sure. Can you give me about five minutes?"

"No problem. Have you had breakfast? I can order something."

"No, thanks. I'm fine. I'll see you in five."

Traci flopped back into her chair and spun it toward the window. She wanted this thing to be over. She wanted to get her old life back. She wanted to get away from Michael and bury the memories and the hurt and humiliation. She pressed her fist to her mouth to keep from screaming. So many times she questioned what she'd done. This was the man she'd loved. But she'd betrayed him like Judas. And she couldn't help but ask herself if it was pure jealousy and a desire for revenge or because she truly believed that what he was doing was wrong.

She slowly stood up. Unfortunately, it was too late to turn back now. All the wheels were in motion and a part of her ached at what the days ahead would hold.

Michael's door was partially open when she arrived. She tapped and poked her head in.

He glanced up from his computer screen and quickly clicked off the page he was on. "Hey, come on in." He got up and walked over to the small island that held the coffee machine. "Coffee?"

"No, thanks." She sat down opposite his desk and noticed the screen saver on his computer.

He poured himself a cup and returned to his desk. "So, let me hear your thoughts about last night."

"I thought it went off without a hitch." She handed over the copies of the early reviews.

He briefly glanced at them, nodding and smiling before setting them aside. "I wanted to thank you for all of your help. Raven was a difficult client to handle, but you made it work."

"Thank you."

He was quiet for a moment. "I want to host a private gathering at my place in the Poconos for some of my clients in two weeks. It will be for the entire weekend."

"Okay. Do you know who you want to invite?"

"I'll put the list of names together and get it to you so you can begin contacting them." He took a sip of his coffee. "I want to use MT Management again."

She didn't respond.

"How do you feel about that?"

"Why should I feel one way or the other?" she said, a bit more harshly than she intended.

"Look, I'm sorry for how things turned out between us. I

shouldn't have led you on all this time, let you think that it could be more than what it was. But you have to know that I do care about you, Brenda, at least as much as I'm capable of caring for anyone. You're an incredible woman. I never wanted to hurt you and I hope that what happened with us isn't going to interfere with us continuing to work together, especially since you've made it clear that…we can't have what we once did."

"What about Mia? Did you only care about her as much as you were capable of caring for anyone?"

He glanced away. "Maybe more than that. But she left me, and with good reason." He sighed heavily. "After that I haven't been able to commit myself to anyone. So…this has nothing to do with you."

"I was just a replacement," she challenged.

He didn't respond.

"I guess that's my answer." She got up. "I need to get some work started on the Pocono event. I'll work with Mia to put it together." She turned to leave.

"Brenda…"

Her hand stilled on the knob of the door.

"I'm sorry."

She straightened her shoulders and walked out.

Within the hour Michael e-mailed her the list of ten men he wanted to invite to the gathering. Even Traci was impressed. She immediately e-mailed the list to Mia. It was up to her now.

Mia was thinking about the information that Traci had e-mailed to her earlier as she prepared dinner. The guest list was staggering. If this final sting panned out, it would rock the city. The list included Senator Max Hopkinson, who was currently running for reelection; CEO Carl Ruthers, founder of Ruthers Technology and the man who had single-handedly revolutionized identity-scanning systems worldwide; and Breck Hamilton, the chairman of Backstreet Records, among others. She couldn't begin to imagine the fallout.

She put two handfuls of mixed greens into the colander, rinsed them then tossed them into a teal-and-white-colored ceramic mixing bowl that she'd picked up on a business jaunt in Mexico a couple of years earlier and began adding her ingredients. She'd already grilled a fresh piece of salmon, which she began to slice into slender pieces. She would add this as the final topping.

The wine was chilled. She had showered and applied body lotion in Steven's favorite scent. She'd slipped into a brand-new Victoria's Secret teddy in a shimmering hot pink that did wonderful things to her skin.

She put the salmon salad in the fridge to chill just a bit, cleaned her fingers—first with lemon juice, followed by warm water and soap, to get rid of the fish smell—then hurried into the living room to lower the lights and put on a CD of the Dells' greatest hits to be followed by her favorite, Luther. But she was pretty sure they'd never be sitting around long enough to actually hear it.

Several small aromatic candles burned in strategic places around the room, enveloping the space in the soft scent of lavender.

Mia took a look around, satisfied with her setup. She planned to give Steven the loving that he deserved and that she wanted. Being with him, being a part of him, seemed to help exorcise Michael from her system and keep at bay the double life that she led. When she was with Steven, she could just be Mia, the neurotic, quirky event planner who refused to wear her glasses. And that was okay.

She smiled at the thought. It had taken almost making a fatal mistake with Michael, having his true side and her own weakness revealed to her for her to realize what it was that she already had. Michael was a fantasy, a passion from her past. Steven was her here, her now and her tomorrow.

As she toweled off her hands, she heard the front door open. She tossed the towel onto the counter, grabbed the wine from the bottom of the fridge, along with the two long-stemmed wineglasses, and met Steven just as he was putting down the briefcase that held his laptop. That's when he spotted the hot-pink beauty in the archway of the kitchen that opened onto the dining and living-room area. He also noticed the low lights, the heady scent of jasmine and the dark look in his woman's eyes.

The corner of his mouth rose ever so slightly. He shrugged out of his jacket and hung it on the coatrack near the closet door. He moved slowly in her direction, as she posed provocatively against the frame of the archway with the two glasses swinging from her hand.

"Hey, handsome," she said, her voice soft and inviting.

Steven walked up to her. "Hey, yourself." He took the bottle from her hand, leaned down and kissed her softly. He uncorked the bottle. She held out the glasses and he poured.

They touched glasses and took their first sip before they both turned to the sound of the Dells' "Stay in My Corner."

Steven tossed his head back and laughed, then looked down into Mia's teasing gaze. "You know that's the jam."

He took the glass from her hand, set his down, along with the bottle of wine, then slipped his arm around her silken waist, pulling her up against him. "Can I have this dance?"

"I'd love to," she whispered.

They moved to the center of the living room and fell into perfect step with each other, swaying to the serious old-school love song. Mia rested her head on Steven's chest as he held her, running his hand up and down along the soft fabric, intermittently cupping her rear to pull her tighter against him.

Mia was on a natural high: the music, the aromas, the man. They all contributed to her feeling of peace, mixed with a sensual heat that made her almost light-headed with the growing need that rushed through her insides, much like the hot flame of a match tossed on kindling.

"I fixed dinner," she murmured against his ear as the song was drawing to its hip-grinding last note, which made the standard a favorite among generations of slow dancers.

"We can bring it inside," he said, nibbling on her neck. He stroked her back, running his hand along the curve of her hip.

"We could. Why don't you get settled and I'll serve you dinner in bed."

"Loving the sound of that." He kissed her and headed off toward the back of the condo.

Moments later, Mia heard the sound of running water. She returned to the kitchen, took out the salad, got plates and silverware and placed them all on the large serving tray that they used when they ate in bed. She added linen napkins, two clean glasses and the bottle of wine. Balancing it all like a professional, she took it to their bedroom and set it all on the side table. She turned back the blanket, fluffed the pillows and dimmed the lights.

Looking around with her hands on her hips, she was satisfied with the ambience.

Michael stepped out of the adjoining bathroom, followed by a rush of steam. He had a towel wrapped around his waist and was drying off his hair and face with another one. When he pulled the towel away from his face, his eyes lit up.

"Woman, you sure know how to welcome a man home from a hard day's work."

Mia sat on the side of the bed, her long legs crossed at the knee. "I try." She patted the space next to her. Steven didn't need to be invited twice. He read her body language very well.

Once he was next to her, she lifted a forkful of the salmon salad to his lips. "Taste."

His eyes closed in what looked like ecstasy. "Hmm, delicious." He chewed slowly.

"Here, have a sip." She held up the glass of wine to his lips.

He took a long swallow, removed the glass from her fingers. He reached around her and filled a fork with the salad and fed her, then offered her a sip of wine.

The entire ritual of feeding each other, the submissiveness of allowing yourself to be fed, and the dominance of being the provider was an intoxicating, sensory turn-on for them both, as the positions of power and vulnerability shifted back and forth between them.

When the food and most of the wine was gone and their roles had blurred, all they wanted to feast on was each other.

Tonight Mia was feeling her feminine power, and as much as she loved Steven taking the lead, tonight was her night. She removed their plates and glasses, setting them back on the tray. She stood in front of him as he gazed up at her, trying to anticipate what she might do.

She reached down and loosened the towel around his waist, then instructed him to take it off and sit back down. When he was seated and she eyed his steadily growing erection, she took the first strap and then the other of her teddy and pushed them down her shoulders and shimmied out of it, allowing the fabric to float into a pink pool at her feet. She stepped over it, draped her legs on either side of Steven's hard thighs. She clasped the back of his head and pulled him flush against the softness of her stomach, allowing him to momentarily inhale the scent that he loved.

She took his hands and lifted them to her breasts, which demanded to be fondled.

Steven cupped them, their ripeness overflowing his palms. He allowed his thumbs to gently graze back and forth across her nipples, the way he knew she liked it.

Mia moaned. For a moment her eyes closed, as she gave

in to the sensual delight that fired through her veins. As he caressed her, she slowly lowered herself onto his hardened shaft, which was pointing toward heaven. As she slid down on the hot thickness of him, her mind spun, her belly was on fire, her heart pumped as she felt her insides open up to welcome him.

She enveloped him to the hilt and, as always, it took a moment for her body to adjust to the solid rock hardness of him, which seemed to grow thicker with every beat of her heart, taking her breath away.

Steven grabbed a handful of her behind in each palm, his mouth replacing where his hands once were.

Mia cried out his name, wrapped her hands around his neck, planted the balls of her feet solidly on the floor and rode him like a seasoned rodeo rider, making Steven holler with pleasure.

Later, they rested in a tangle of sheets and limbs, talking softly to each other about their workday, when Steven sprang his surprise.

"This is the kind of time we need to spend together," he began.

"Hmm, umm," she mumbled against his chest. She ran a manicured finger down the center.

"I know we are both crazy busy with work, so I figured the only real alone time we're going to have is if we get away somewhere."

Her eyes opened slowly.

"That's why I went ahead and got us two tickets for a Bahamas weekend getaway, everything included. I knew if we kept talking about when we have some free time to do something, it would never happen. So I got us tickets for two weeks from now. We leave on Thursday and come back on Sunday. That will give us both some time to prepare staff, get anything important out of the way."

"Weekend after next?" She was paying attention now.

"Yep, all paid for."

Mia's stomach knotted. It was the same weekend as the Poconos. What the hell was she going to do?

Chapter 21

Mia barely slept. Her eyes were wide-open when the sun crested the horizon. All she could think about all night was her dilemma. How damn Twilight Zone was it that Steven had bought tickets to the Bahamas for the same freaking weekend as Michael's getaway weekend for his "special" friends. Her eyes felt as if someone had shoveled sand under her lids, but she couldn't lie in bed a minute longer.

While Steven was still sound asleep, she tiptoed into the kitchen with her cell phone pressed to her chest and, checking to make sure he hadn't awakened, she dialed the girls, leaving urgent messages on all their cell phones. They needed an emergency meeting ASAP.

Mia did all she could not to push Steven out the door. Today of all days he wanted to linger, talk, make love again…and again. Any other time, she would have been all for it, but she had cases to crack and people to see.

Sometime during the night it had rained. The streets

were still wet, with water pooling in the numerous inden-
tations of New York City sidewalks and streets. By the
time she reached her car, which she'd parked on the next
block, she felt as if she'd completed the Olympic hurdles.
Her condo had a parking facility attached to the building—
and well it should, for all the money the tenants shelled
out—but she'd never bothered to take advantage of it, especially during the spring and summer. Parking around
the corner or down the block gave her a chance to get in
her minimal amount of exercise. Steven had practically
begged her to use the parking garage, especially because
she had so many late nights, but she'd been adamant. The
winter would be there soon enough, she'd explained, and
she would be forced to park in the garage and take the
elevator, and so that would bring an end to her meager
attempt at fitness.

Once behind the wheel, she turned on the radio to keep her
company and to keep her mind off her newest dilemma. The
Steve Harvey Morning Show was on, and one of the hosts was
tearing into some poor soul about discovering that her man
had a whole other family on the other side of a very small
town in North Carolina.

Mia just shook her head and chuckled. If only she could
write to Steve about her ongoing drama. She'd pay good
money to hear what he had to say about it. He'd probably tell
her that she was lying about the whole mess.

What she really needed was Danielle and Savannah's
input. They'd always given her sound advice and now that
they knew the whole story, she was sure they'd be objective.
She'd even invited Ashley, whose personality was a nice fit
for their group. The fact that she, too, was a Cartel member
only strengthened the bond.

Unfortunately, bad weather brought out the worst drivers.
They suddenly became totally inept at moving from point A to

point B with any degree of speed. The ultimate result was that Mia's fifteen-minute ride turned into a half hour of stop and go.

Finally, she reached The Shop and, shock of all shocks, Danielle, the queen of "Janie Come Lately," had actually arrived first and was holding down their favorite booth. She really must be off her game, Mia thought as she moved toward the table, especially if Danielle of all people was the first to arrive anywhere. Maybe the moon was in Aquarius or something.

"Hey, girl, what in the hell are you doing here so early?" She sat down and slid across the booth on her side until she reached the end. She placed her purse between her and the partition.

"I'm trying to turn over a new leaf," Danielle confessed. "Being early, less cussing, listening before speaking, being considerate of others." She took a sip of tea.

Mia sat there with her eyes wide with disbelief. "You're kidding me, right?"

Danielle made a face. "No. For real."

"Why?" Mia asked, totally perplexed. "We're already used to you being a tactless, late, pain in the neck, supersweet friend. If it ain't broke, don't fix it."

"I think that was some kind of compliment, but I'm not sure."

"Did Nick get on you about something?"

"No. Actually during a photo shoot, one of the product placement items was this book, *Twenty Days to a Better You.* During the break I checked it out and figured, why not?" She shrugged lightly.

"Hmm. How's it going so far?"

"Got me here early." She grinned. "But it's too soon to tell. Somebody piss me off and it's on."

They laughed just as Savannah and Ashley pushed through the door, both shaking out their umbrellas. A flash of lightning was followed by a roll of thunder.

"Damn, I thought this kind of weather was reserved for April," Savannah groused as she kissed cheeks, slid out of her raincoat and sat down.

"Hey, y'all," Ashley greeted them. She fluffed her fro and hung her jacket on the back of the booth chair. She turned to Mia. "So what's up and who's paying for breakfast?"

"Now that's what I'm talking about," Danielle said. "I knew I liked you for a reason. Straight, no chaser."

"Well, since I called the meeting, I guess I'll pay for breakfast," Mia said. She flitted her hand around the table, as if sprinkling fairy dust. "But everyone choose something different. That way I can charge it as a business expense." She grinned.

Danielle and Savannah shook their heads. Mia was notorious for finding creative ways to use her business account.

"So, sister girl, what's the story?" Savannah asked.

Mia drew in a long breath then leaned forward. "Well, you all know that Michael is planning a private party."

Nodding heads all around.

"Last night—"

"What can I get you ladies this morning?" the waitress asked, cutting Mia off.

They each placed their orders—everything from egg-white omelets to Belgian waffles. Once the waitress was gone, Mia continued.

"Steven and I…well, we had a fantastic night." She blushed and the girls humm-ummed her, knowing just what she meant. "So afterward we were lying there, and I'm thinking, 'Yes, this is where I want to be, where my heart is,' ya know, and he starts telling me that we really need more time like this together without a lot of distractions…blah, blah, blah. So I'm all for it. Sounding really good, right. Then BAM. He drops an atom bomb. He got us two round-trip tickets to the Bahamas."

"Whoa. You go, girl," Ashley said.

"That's what I'm talking about," Danielle added.

"I hear a *but* in there somewhere," said Savannah, always the astute one.

"A big one. The tickets are for the exact same weekend as the private party."

"Daayum," they chorused, turning the one word into two.

"Talk about bad timing," Ashley said.

"I have no idea what to do. I have to be up in the Poconos."

"You need to go with Steven," Savannah said emphatically.

"I agree," Danielle said.

"But how am I going to explain my absence to Michael?"

"You don't. I'll take your place," Savannah said.

"What?"

"We'll make it work. Danielle is already one of the ladies. I'm helping out because you're ill. I'll work it out with Traci. Ashley had to cover one of your other events." She shrugged her shoulders and held her palms facing the ceiling. "Simple."

Mia looked from one expectant face to other. "Do you really think he'd go for it?"

"What choice does he have?" Danielle said. "You don't tell him jack until the last second. By then all the players are in place."

Mia nodded slowly. "I can't jeopardize what Steven and I have. I just can't. I cringe to think I was involved with a man who could do what he's doing." She gave a slight shiver.

"Let's be honest. Michael Burke is fine, charming, intelligent, well-off. What woman wouldn't fall for him?" Savannah said. "And, to be honest, I really believe he cared for you and still does. But that doesn't excuse what he's done and is still doing. Besides, if he would cheat on his wife, one of these days he'd do the same thing to you."

For a moment Mia looked crestfallen. Hearing the hard truth was definitely a reality check. "Let's work this plan, then," she finally conceded. "I'm sure this will be my last assignment once Jean finds out that I opted to pursue my love life instead of my job."

"Jean will get over it," Ashley said. "If she can take Traci back into the fold, she'll do the same for you."

"I sure hope so."

Danielle and her fiancé, Nick, decided to take in a movie instead of going home after the end of their day of shooting.

"I think things went pretty well today," Nick said as they stood in line waiting for tickets to Denzel's latest movie.

Danielle hooked her arm through Nick's. It had taken her a while to feel comfortable expressing her feelings for Nick in public. For one thing, they worked together. And then there was the whole race thing. Although both of them—in the animal kingdom—would be considered mutts for their mixed breeding, Danielle had always lived as a black girl in an "I'm not sure what she is" body. Nick, on the other hand, grew up as a white boy with white-boy privileges, even though his heart and soul were darker than hers.

But none of that mattered anymore. She'd made her peace with herself and, more important, with her family—her dad, in particular—and ever since then she had felt as if the weight of the world had been lifted from her shoulders.

"Fortunately, everything was in studio. I'm hoping tomorrow is better. We have the shots to take for the winter coat line for JCPenney."

"I know. We'll improvise."

Nick paid for their tickets and they walked inside, both heading straight for the popcorn. They turned to each other and grinned. Popcorn was the thing that had broken the employer/employee ice between them. Danielle was a fiend for popcorn. She could never turn it down. And one afternoon during a photo shoot on Long Island, Nick had whipped out a bag of popcorn and Danielle had begun to salivate. When

Nick offered her some, she nearly screamed yes. As they shared the oversize bag, they started talking, finding that they had tons of things in common: music, movies, books, neighborhoods, musicians, architecture. It was amazing and the rest, as they say, is history—in the making.

"Make sure you ask for extra butter, 'cause I ain't sharing," Nick said.

Danielle rolled her eyes.

They placed their orders and walked into the darkened theater. They had about ten minutes before the feature presentation, so they settled down to watch the previews. It was Nick who changed the direction of their inconsequential conversation.

"So what's new with the Cartel?" he asked.

On her last case, Danielle had broken one of the cardinal rules of the Cartel; she'd told Nick some details after he discovered her kit. Not everything, but enough for him to know that she had "another life," one that she wouldn't always share with him. Actually, he'd had a hand in her last case, which had involved identity theft.

"It's Mia's case this time," she said, before shoving a handful of popcorn in her mouth.

"Anything you can talk about?"

"I wasn't supposed to say that," she said, with a hint of laughter in her voice.

"My bad."

"All I can say is that it's major. There's a party coming up soon. Very exclusive. Very highbrow guests."

"I can mingle," Nick said. "Something like that you need a bartender, right?" He grinned into the darkness. "I'm your man."

She munched on her popcorn. "I'll let you know. But don't count on it."

"Party pooper."

She poked him in the side with her elbow. Relaxing in

her seat, she was amazed at how far they'd come. Both of them had struggled with intimacy issues, trusting another person totally. But once she finally opened her heart and spirit to Nick, everything changed. She relished the fact that she could trust him with her darkest secrets, even being a member of the Cartel. That level of trust brought them closer. She glanced down at the diamond sparkling on the third finger of her left hand. Yes, things had definitely changed for the better. And, if need be, she would certainly take Nick up on his offer. Nothing like having two spies in the family.

Mia dreaded what she was about to do, but she had no choice. Throughout the night, she'd struggled with what she would say and how Jean would react. But truth be told, she'd rather jeopardize her standing with the Cartel than with Steven.

She parked her car across the street from the brownstone. For several moments she sat behind the wheel, rehearsing in her head what she was going to say. She watched the comings and goings of the men attending the Pause for Men Spa. One of these days she was going to pay the spa a visit just to see what all the hype was about.

Unable to stall any longer, she took off her glasses, tucked them in the glove compartment, grabbed her coat and got out.

Claudia answered the door.

"Good morning, sweetheart."

"Hi, Claudia."

"You don't sound happy."

"I'm not looking forward to my conversation with Jean."

Claudia patted her shoulder. "Whatever it is, I'm sure it will work out. Jean really isn't as bad as everyone thinks."

"Thanks. I'll keep that in mind while she chews off my head," she said, laughing derisively. "And we really need to get together to talk about your wedding plans."

"I know. Time is flying by. But we'll make time to talk once you're finished with your assignment."

"That might be sooner than you think." She took a deep breath. "Wish me luck." She headed upstairs.

When she'd called earlier to tell Jean that she needed to speak with her in person, she got a sense that Jean already knew what she was coming to say. She walked down the hall of fame until she reached Jean's office. She knocked on the door.

"Come in."

Jean barely looked up when Mia came in.

"Have a seat."

Mia's throat was suddenly bone-dry. She thought she might suffocate.

"You wanted to talk. I'm listening." She peered at Mia through the lenses of her red-framed glasses.

Mia cleared her dry throat. "I'm not going to be able to handle the event in the Poconos…"

She went on to explain, as best she could, her current circumstances. She laid out plan B, which had the approval of Savannah and Danielle.

While Mia rambled on about the whys and wherefores of her predicament, Jean didn't move, didn't seem to blink, didn't appear to breathe. Mia was certain that at any moment Jean was simply going to implode.

Stumbling toward the finish line, she wrapped up her monologue and awaited Jean's verdict. She'd resigned herself to the notion that she would be kicked to the curb. However, Jean's response was more devastating than she imagined.

Slowly, Jean removed her glasses and set them down in front of her on the desk. She zeroed in on Mia, making her squirm in her seat.

"The downfall of some of my best operatives has been over a relationship. If you intend to succeed, you must find a way to separate the two. I'm disappointed in you, Mia. But I know that Savannah and Danielle can handle it. They've proven themselves."

Mia felt physically stung by the barb.

"Do what you must." She put her glasses back on and returned to what she was doing before Mia came in.

Mia took that as her cue to leave. And as far as she was concerned, she couldn't get out of there fast enough.

She couldn't even face Claudia so she hurried out and practically sprinted to her car.

Hot tears of defeat and frustration filled her eyes. She'd failed before she'd gotten started. She lowered her head to the steering wheel and let the tears fall. She wasn't a quitter. Her entire life was built on organization and thinking outside the box. She was analytical by nature. And she'd somehow let what came easy to her get away from her. She'd allowed herself to get distracted and out of focus.

She had to return to what came natural to her. Planning.

Chapter 22

Mia took her time getting to her office. At this point, she felt her day could only go from bad to worst. Throughout the ride downtown, she played out a variety of scenarios to make the impossible possible—everything from going with Steven to the Bahamas, buying an extra ticket and flying back to New York then returning to the island. That, of course, was beyond ridiculous. How would she ever explain her absence to Steven for hours on end? She'd even considered telling Steven everything—except the part about her and Michael's past—and taking him with her to the Poconos then flying off to the Bahamas. But she was already on the blacklist with Jean. The last thing she needed to do was involve Steven.

She eventually dragged herself into her office, feeling as gloomy as the overcast day.

"Can't be that bad," Ashley said, upon seeing her distraught expression.

Mia shrugged out of her coat and draped it across her arm. "It is."

"What happened?"

"She told me I was a disappointment and that she was sure that Savannah and Danielle could handle the assignment. After all, *they'd* proven themselves."

Ashley grimaced. "Ouch. Sorry. Look she's probably disappointed, sure, but she'll get over it. The Cartel will be there with or without us, but we have to have a life, too. If I was in your shoes, I'd do the same thing…if that's any consolation."

Mia half smiled. "Thanks." She sighed heavily. "Any messages?"

"Not sure if you want to hear it, but Michael called to remind you about lunch."

Her day had just gotten worst.

Michael had made reservations for them at the Russian Tea Room—pretty swanky for a simple lunch. But she wasn't buying so no need to complain. Hopefully, the serene and upscale atmosphere, suffused with old-world charm, would have enough of an ambience to lift her dour mood and help her get through an hour or more in Michael's presence.

She arrived at one-thirty and was shown immediately to her table. He must come here often, Mia thought as she was ushered toward the back. The moment she said she was meeting Michael Burke for lunch, the hostess's bright blue eyes lit up. At this point, unfortunately, Mia couldn't tell if the recognition was due to Michael's standing in the business community or if this young girl was part of his stable of escorts.

As she approached their somewhat secluded booth, Michael spotted her. A slow smile—the one that creased the corners of his eyes and did something to her insides that she was never able to explain or understand—moved across his mouth, showing just a hint of teeth.

Her heart knocked hard in her chest, forcing the blood to rush to her head. For an instant she felt dizzy, as if she were about to swoon like the ladies sitting on a Charleston porch at the height of summer, sipping mint julips.

He extended his hand to her and she found herself enveloped in its warmth. He slid his other lightly around her waist, then kissed her gently on the cheek before helping her into her chair as the heady scent of his cologne short-circuited her thoughts.

The moment she sat, she reached for the glass of water and took several swallows as Michael swung back into his seat opposite her.

At least the water had a cooling effect and she slowly began to clear her head. Michael always had that power over her, to be able to seduce her mind and body with no more effort than simply being in her space. His smile, his touch, the scent of him were all aphrodisiacs, and even after all these years that combination was still as potent as it had ever been.

That was what kept her on the fence. That was what made her so indecisive and hesitant. She wanted him to be the Michael she knew—an adulterer, certainly—but not a common pimp.

"Thanks for coming," he said, the familiar timbre of his voice snapping her out of her musings. "I appreciate it."

"I try to accommodate my business clients as much as possible." She folded her hands in her lap.

The waitress appeared to take their drink and food orders.

Michael ordered wine and a Caesar salad, Mia a bottle of Pellegrino and grilled salmon salad. They returned the menus to the waitress.

"I must tell you again how impressed I was with the red-carpet event. The calls haven't stopped coming in about what a great time everyone had."

Mia nodded and smiled. "It's what I do."

"You were always good," he said, his voice lowering to a tone too intimate for a business lunch.

Mia adjusted herself in her seat and took out her notepad. "So, what did you want to talk to me about?" she asked, trying to stay focused.

The right corner of his mouth rose upward for a split second. "All work and no play…"

"Michael—"

"Okay, okay." He clasped his hands on top of the table and Mia couldn't help but notice the fresh manicure and the way his long fingers laced in and out of each other. "My house in the Poconos is fine for the party. There's plenty of space. I think it would still make sense for you to come up and take a look first."

Mia made a note then returned her gaze to Michael.

The waitress reappeared with their drinks order and food.

"However," he continued, "my guests will be…staying over for the weekend. They are going to need accommodations in the immediate area. So I will need ten suites reserved."

The light bulb went off. That was her opening! "I'll take care of it and ensure that your guests have only the best. I'll need a list of their preferences and any special requests."

"Of course. I'll make sure that Brenda gets that information to you as soon as possible, as well as the catering menu. We'll need some entertainment as well. I was thinking a small jazz band."

Mia's mind was racing. She just might be able to pull this off after all. "Of course. I know just the band. They'll be perfect."

Michael took a sip of his drink before focusing on his salad. He stabbed the fork into his food then stopped. "Tell me why you've been avoiding…us."

Her stomach rose and fell. "What are you talking about?"

"Us." He suddenly covered her hand with his. "Please don't pull away. Just hear me out. I know I made mistakes. I should never have cheated on my wife and had you living the kind of life that wasn't worthy of you." He paused. "I never saw you as the other woman—but as *my* woman, the one I wanted to be with. But by the time I got my act together, you were gone. I'd give it all up, everything, the business, the deals…other women if I could have you."

"Michael, too much time has passed."

"Enough to heal the hurts, the disappointments?"

She looked away.

"All I ask is that you give me a chance—one chance to prove to you that I've changed. Please."

"How are you going to do that?"

"You'll see. After the party, you'll see."

Mia stared at his bowed head as he ate his food. *What did he mean?*

She shouldn't even be entertaining Michael's thinly veiled proposition. He always had a way of making her see and believe what he wanted. That was his strength and her weakness. But there was no time for weakness, not now, she thought as she maneuvered her car around the late-afternoon traffic.

After he'd made his declaration, he'd steered clear of anything else on a personal level. They talked about politics, the upcoming election and what it could mean for the country. They talked about movies, music, all the things they had in common, and for a while she totally forgot that this could never be. For a while she was the old Mia Turner who was totally enamored of the dashing Michael Burke. That was then, she reminded herself, reliving the easy banter that had characterized their past relationship. No place for memories now, she reminded herself as she pulled into the last parking spot on the block.

Yet, his statement clung to her like a static-charged skirt against panty hose without a slip. And as much as she tried to disconnect the electricity that drew the skirt to the hose, she couldn't. It just kept on clinging, riding up and down her thigh, making her uncomfortable.

Mia turned off the ignition and got out. She glanced skyward. Dark clouds still hovered threateningly over the city. Even though it was only October, it felt like snow. Shivering slightly, she pulled her coat around her and hurried toward her office.

"Getting really cold out there," she said in a huff as she came inside.

"I was listening to the news. They're expecting the temperature to drop into the twenties tonight."

Mia grumbled.

"So how did it go?"

Mia's brows rose. "I think I may have found a way." She pulled up a chair near Ashley's desk and detailed her plan.

"Sounds like it just might work."

Mia got up. "I'm going to start making some calls."

Mia brought her electronic Rolodex up on her computer. Her business and reputation were built on who she knew, and Mia knew everyone who mattered. She pulled up her list of resorts, then began sorting them by location. There were three in the Pocono area. The first call didn't pan out. There were not enough rooms free. The second call was another bust. The manager was unavailable and the assistant sounded as if she was still in training. Mia tossed up a silent prayer and made her third call.

"Mt. Pocono Resort and Lodge," the young voice answered.

"Good afternoon. My name is Mia Turner of MT Management. I want to arrange a gathering for a party of ten."

"Hold on. Let me get you the booking manager."

Mia nervously tapped her foot as she waited. A few moments later a male voice came on the line.

"Mia?"

"Yes."

"Mia, it's Leon Winston."

Her eyes widened in surprise. "Leon! Oh, my goodness. When did you move out of the city?"

He chuckled. "Actually, I didn't. I stay up here during the week and come down to the city on weekends. How in the world are you?"

She'd worked with Leon several times over the years. He'd been a manager at the Hilton for ages. The last time they'd worked together was on a celebrity party.

"I'm doing well. Busy but good."

"So what can I do for you?"

"It's a bit complicated, but I need to book ten suites for three weeks from now."

"Wow, cutting it close. But we're just outside of the winter season…hmm, hang on."

Mia's heart pumped. This was her last shot.

Leon came back on the phone. "We can make it work."

She exhaled a major breath of relief. "You are a lifesaver."

"For you, anything."

"There's something else."

"Shoot."

"Should anyone call you and ask why the suites weren't booked for the weekend after next, just say that they were unavailable."

"Not a problem."

Mia shut her eyes in relief. "Great. Thanks so much. Shoot me an invoice and I'll get the payment out to you."

"Sure thing."

"And, Leon, thanks."

"That's what friends are for. I'll e-mail you a link to the resort. You'll be able to take a virtual tour, get a sense of the space. Any questions, just call me."

"Will do. Take care, Leon."

"You, too. Thanks for the business."

She flopped back into her seat. Mission accomplished. She smiled in triumph. There was only one glitch. If anything was to go down, it had to take place at Michael's home. There was no way that she was going to involve her friend, Leon. She didn't want his business—or hers—connected to the sting.

She pushed up from her seat and went out to bring Ashley up-to-date.

Ashley shook her head in amazement, a big grin stretching across her mouth. "I knew you'd find a way."

"Let's just hope that it works. No more surprises."

Chapter 23

She knew he was going to be upset. Michael was accustomed to having his way—all the time. However, she was shocked by the explosion of his temper.

"Three weeks!" His voice boomed through the phone, rocking Mia back in her seat. "I didn't say three weeks, Mia. I specifically said two and for a damn good reason. This is unacceptable. You're going to have to change it. Now! And if you can't, I'll get someone else to handle this."

She gripped the phone to keep her hands from shaking. The last thing she needed was him flying off the handle and getting someone else to take over the assignment. She couldn't let that happen.

"Then get someone else," she said, combating his tirade with cool calm. "I'm sure you can find someone much more capable than me. And that someone else will tell you exactly what I just did—there is nothing available in your area for the week you wanted unless you want your very special guests to bunk together. So, since you will no longer be needing my services…have a good day, Michael."

She drew in a breath, threw up a silent prayer.

"Wait."

Her entire body trembled as she waited.

"Yes?"

"Look, I'm sorry. I'm sure you did everything you could."

Mia could almost see his face contorting as he apologized. "So what are you saying?"

She heard him mutter a curse through the phone.

"Three weeks."

She hoped he couldn't hear the thudding of her heart. "Fine. I'll get right on it."

He hung up without saying goodbye, which was fine with Mia. Less chance for the wrong thing to be said.

It was time for a meeting of the minds.

The Shop was cozy and warm when Mia arrived, accompanied by Ashley. By the time they were settled and had ordered a plate of buffalo wings as appetizers, Savannah came in, her short hairdo slightly windswept around her cupie-doll face.

"Hey, ladies," Savannah greeted them, shrugging out of her coat. "Is it just us?"

"Dani should be here shortly. She had a shoot to finish that was running late. And I invited Traci."

"Oh," they chorused.

As if on cue, Traci came through the door, spotted the trio and headed in their direction.

"Hey, everybody."

"Hi." She looked around hesitantly.

"Have a seat, girl," Savannah offered.

Traci took off her coat and slid in next to Ashley. She folded her hands on top of the table. "Thanks for inviting me. I know this is kinda y'all's thing."

"Always room for one more," Mia said and offered a smile. Traci took a seat next to Savannah.

"Hope you like buffalo wings," Ashley said, digging in.

"Yep." She picked one up from the plate.

"I want to wait until Dani gets here so that I don't have to say everything twice."

Savannah picked up a wing and dipped it in the blue cheese dressing, just as Danielle blew in on a blast of chilly air.

"Now the party can get started," she said in greeting. She squeezed in next to Traci. "Nice to see you here."

"Thanks."

"Let's get all the business out of the way and then we can eat, drink and be merry," Mia said.

"Now that's what I'm talking about," Danielle chimed.

Mia told them what she'd been able to pull off for the Pocono weekend, the juggling of the weekend date and having Leon back her up, should he ever be questioned.

"Don't ever let anybody tell you that you don't know the people who count," Danielle teased.

Mia winked. "So now I can spend time with my man, put the screws to my ex and hang with my girls. Who could ask for more?"

They all laughed.

"Of course, Ashley, you are going to have to be on the outside. I need you to photograph everyone coming in and out of there."

"Got it."

"Dani, you'll be one of the girls."

"Oh, guess I should have mentioned that Michelle called me this afternoon to tell me that Michael wanted me to be there."

"Great. Savannah, you'll run point—eyes and ears—girl."

"Not a problem."

"Traci, you have your end covered. We'll be working together."

Traci nodded.

"We'll stay in touch and Traci will keep us up-to-date on any changes from inside." Mia sat back. "We're good?"

"Yep."

"So enough about business. Let's talk beaches and moonlit nights," Savannah urged.

Mia laughed. "I can't wait," she said, her expression lighting up. "I can't remember the last time I was away that didn't have something to do with my job or a client."

"Make the most of it," Danielle said. "The good times are few and far between."

"I wish Blake and I could get away," Savannah said, "but I can't bear to leave Mikayla. Going to work is bad enough."

"How old is she?" Traci asked.

"Six months." She dug in her purse and whipped out her wallet, bulging with photos.

"Oh, boy," her trio of friends groaned.

"Don't get her started on Mikayla," Danielle teased. "We'll be talking about Pampers, baby bottles and how brilliant her baby is for the rest of the night."

Savannah waved her hand in dismissal and proceeded to show Traci pictures of her bundle of joy.

The waitress came to take their orders and the ladies continued their conversation, talking about their love lives, jobs, the latest books they'd read and what movie star they'd love to meet.

Before they knew it, it was nearly nine o'clock.

"I really have got to go," Savannah said. "Blake will start blowing up my cell phone in a minute and I want to give Mikayla her last feeding." She got up and prepared to leave.

"Me, too," Danielle said. "This has been great, as usual."

Mia reached for the check.

"No. Let me get it," Traci said. "My way of saying thanks."

All the ladies turned questioning gazes on Traci.

"I really appreciate y'all including me. It's been a long time since I had real girlfriends." She looked at each of them.

"We're glad to have you," Savannah said. She squeezed her shoulder.

"Damn, girl, if I knew you were paying, I would have ordered drinks!" Danielle teased. "Welcome to the club," she said, her tone serious but welcoming.

"Thanks."

"Be sure to take plenty of pictures," Savannah said as she waved goodbye.

"I want audio," Ashley said.

Ashley stood. "Just have a good time, girl. This mess will be here waiting when you get back."

If she knew nothing else, that was definitely true. Mia got her coat and purse and followed her friends out into the night.

Chapter 24

Steven had spared no expense for this trip. He'd refused to tell her where they were staying. But the trip started off with them flying first class, being picked up by a driver at the airport and then taken to Sandals Resorts.

The driver opened Mia's door and she stepped out with her mouth open. She spun toward Steven and flew into his arms.

"Sandals," she squealed.

"Couples only," he said into her hair as he swung her around.

She wiggled up against him, reached up and kissed him tenderly on the lips. "Thank you," she whispered against his mouth.

"For what?" He brushed some hair away from her face.

"For doing this for us."

"Lady, you ain't seen nothing yet." He swept her up in his arms and carried her laughing and giggling into the hotel lobby.

Once they checked in and were escorted to their room, Mia was shocked once again. The room was magnificent, with a terrace that overlooked the ocean, a sprawling sunken living room, full kitchen, master bedroom and bath. The décor was pure island bliss. Sheer white drapery wafted in the windows, low-slung furniture in bamboo and white canvas dotted the gleaming wood floors. The scent of clear blue ocean water settled all around them.

Mia turned in a slow circle, taking in the space. "This is beautiful," she said softly, turning to face Steven, who watched her as if awestruck. "What is it?"

"You. You're the one that's beautiful." He crossed the short distance between them and took her hands. "I want us to have the best time. Anything you want, whatever you want to do for the next three days."

A devilish grin teased her mouth. "How 'bout we test out that king-size bed for starters?"

"You don't have to ask me twice."

After they'd christened the bed, they took a shower together then ordered room service and ate on the terrace under the stars, a traditional island meal of flying fish, plantains and seasoned callaloo, with mouthwatering mango sherbet for dessert.

Following dinner, which was accompanied by strains of calypso music in the distance, the crash of waves against the shore and the unmistakable sound of voices on the beach enjoying the glorious night, they decided to take a walk and get a feel for the island they'd heard so much about but had never had the chance to visit.

They strolled along the beach, holding hands, something they rarely had a chance or the time to do. The balmy air was intoxicating, and they felt light and carefree.

"I can't believe how good I feel after only being here for

a few hours," Mia said, leaning against Steven as they walked along the sand.

"It is kinda magical. Must be the sea air and the sense of being worry free. I haven't seen anyone rushing, looking stressed or using a BlackBerry."

Mia laughed. "You're absolutely right. It's a completely different world." She stopped, pulled him to her. "And I love it. I love you."

He threaded his fingers through her loose hair, lowered his head and slowly took her mouth to his. His insides seemed to fill, his heart raced and an exquisite sense of peace flowed through him. He caressed her back, holding her close. This was paradise, he thought as his tongue played with hers. Paradise was being with the one woman who made waking up every day an adventure, filled with limitless possibility.

The following day Mia and Steven went into town and spent the entire day window-shopping, shopping for real and sampling all the island foods that their stomachs could hold. They stopped and listened to a steel drum band on a street corner. Open-air shops with tantalizing trinkets beckoned them.

By the time they returned to their hotel, they were weighted down with bags, having bought souvenirs for all their friends and loads of knickknacks for their condo.

"We're going to pay through the nose to get all this stuff back," Mia said as she unpacked their spoils. "We'll need another suitcase just for all the things we bought."

"I know. But it was worth it. I had a great time today. What about you?" He pulled his shirt over his head and tossed it on a lounge chair near the window.

Mia plopped spread-eagle on the bed. "I'm having a ball. We definitely must do this more often."

"All we have to do is make it happen. I have a surprise for you for tonight."

She sprung up. "What?"

He angled his head to the side and wagged his finger at her. "If I told you—"

"It wouldn't be a surprise," she finished for him and plopped back down, this time adding a pout.

"Making faces won't get me to talk."

She folded her arms defiantly. "Fine."

"Just wear something light and pretty. That's all you need to know."

Mia had purchased an entire new wardrobe for their mini-vacation. She stood in the doorway of the bedroom closet contemplating what to wear. She decided on a burnt-orange sundress made of a gauze material that was as light as air and kissed her ankles. She pulled her shoulder-length hair up into a loose knot on top of her head, added simple gold hoops in her ears and a dash of lipstick. Slipping into a pair of sandals, she was ready.

"Perfect," Steven said from behind her.

She turned. "You like?"

"Very much." He came up to her and ran his hand along the fabric of her dress, the heat of her skin coming right through the thin material. "It's going to be hard concentrating on dinner when I know that you have nothing on underneath this dress," he said, his voice growing thick.

"Try," she whispered. "It will make it more fun later."

He hooked his arm around her waist and nuzzled her neck until she moaned in delight. He gave her a quick kiss in that hot spot on her neck before releasing her.

When they reached the lobby, they were met by the concierge.

"Your car is right out front, Mr. Long."

"Thank you."

"Car? Where are we going?"

"Surprise, remember?" He took her hand and led her outside to the waiting car.

Mia got in beside him. "Do you even know how to drive on the wrong side of the street?" She buckled up.

Steve chuckled. "We'll see."

Mia held on and they took off.

Driving through the narrow, busy streets was a test of nerves and certainly skill. But Steven was cool, calm and collected as he wove his way around the dirt and cobblestone roads.

The evening was picture-perfect. The sky was absolutely clear, with sparkling stars dusting the sky, and the moon hung at a precarious angle, joining the constellations in brilliance. A gentle ocean breeze cooled the air and carried the intoxicating scents of island foods and fruits.

Soon, Mia realized that they were driving out of the town proper and little by little there were fewer people and buildings to see. Now all that was in view were scattered cottages and a few strollers walking along the beach.

Finally, Steven brought the car to a stop near a cove of trees tucked away from what was left of civilization.

"Where are we and how in the world did you find this place?" Mia asked as she unbuckled her seat belt and got out.

"I asked around," he teased. He went to the trunk of the car and opened it, pulling out a huge basket. He shut the trunk door, came around to Mia and took her hand. "Come on."

"Is that what I think it is?" she asked, excitement lighting her voice when she saw the oversize basket.

"We'll have to see, won't we?"

He led them to an even more secluded place along the beach, protected by what looked like a small cave and beautiful foliage. He set the basket down, opened the top and pulled out a blue-and-white blanket that he spread over the sand, followed by a bottle of wine, and dish after dish of island delicacies. To top it off he took out a small radio and tuned it to the local station that was playing sensual island beats.

Mia was awed. "I can't believe you did all this," she said as Steven handed her a glass of wine.

"It wasn't easy sneaking phone calls and making arrangements when we were together just about every minute. Why do you think I was taking so many showers?" he joked. "The hotel must have thought I was nuts. Every time I called there was the sound of rushing water in the background and I was always whispering."

Mia tossed her head back and laughed. "I can only imagine."

"To us," he said, raising his glass to hers.

She touched his glass with her own. "To us. And many more exquisite nights under the stars," she said on a breath, gazing heavenward.

They sampled each of the dishes that the hotel kitchen had specially prepared, talked of inconsequential things, childhood faux pas, the state of the world and when they planned to take another trip together.

After they finished eating, they decided to walk off their meal with a stroll along the beach. Leaving their shoes behind, they waded in and out of the water, darting among the waves as the sand slid from beneath their feet, threatening to take them along for a ride.

"When I was kid," Steven began, "I guess I was about eight, the closest I'd ever come to water outside of the bathtub was the community pool in Philadelphia, where I grew up. I remember one hot-ass summer day my dad took my brother and me to the pool. I couldn't swim, but my father was determined to make me learn." His expression grew pensive in the moonlight as the memories came rushing back.

"I just couldn't seem to get it right and my dad was getting more and more frustrated. I started crying because he was so angry. Then, out of the blue, he smacked me. Smacked me so hard he knocked me down."

Mia gasped and gripped his hand tighter.

"Everyone was staring. A woman tried to intercede, and I remember my dad dared her to try and she backed off, shaking her head and muttering under her breath. Then he turned on me. Told me what a weakling I was, a crybaby. How could I be *his* son? Real men don't whine and cry."

Mia felt his pain and humiliation as if it were her own.

"We finally left the pool and all I could think about was that I wanted to disappear. But when we got in the car, my dad wiped my nose, patted me on the head and told me he was sorry. I was so shocked and confused I didn't know what to say. He went on to tell me that he had to do what he did because I had to be tough, I had to be strong. Especially as a black man. You can't show emotion or become attached to anything or anyone—especially a woman."

He drew in a breath and slowly exhaled, as if trying to physically exorcise the ugly memories.

"He didn't elaborate on it that day, but he did as I got older. Never let a woman know that you care. Never show her emotion. They'll trap you, and once they trap your heart, you're done. And ain't no hurt like the kind of hurt a woman can put on a man."

"My God, how cynical. How could he try to put those kinds of thoughts in your head?"

Steven chuckled sadly. "The really sad part is I believed it. I lived it. But being around Blake and Savannah began to change me. I saw how they were with each other, how they truly cared for each other. I wanted that. I wanted more than just physical intimacy. I wanted to be touched inside." He swallowed back the sudden knot in his throat. "Damn, I sound like just the guy my father never wanted me to be."

Mia stopped walking. She turned him to face her. "But that's the man I want. I never realized just how much until the night you told me 'something almost happened,' and I thought I was losing you. We all have our baggage—I know I do—but we can get through anything if we work at it. I never thought I could be this happy. And, yes, there have been times when I've had my doubts, but you've never given me a reason to doubt the kind of man you are or doubt that your truly care for me and about me." She stroked his cheek then cupped it in her palm. "You're a good man. A hardworking, honest, intelligent, fine, sexy, black man." Her eyes darkened. "I'm getting turned on just talking about you," she said in a throaty whisper.

He leaned down and kissed her slow and deep, the water lapping at their ankles, the moon silhouetting them against the night. "We can do something about that." He brushed his thumb across her nipples, which rose to hard peaks, making her shiver in delight.

"Here?" she asked against his probing mouth.

He looked around. "Nothing watching us but the stars."

Mia giggled. "Race you back to the blanket." She pulled her dress over her head and took off toward the blanket with Steven hot on her heels.

Chapter 25

The week leading up to the event in the Poconos was a constant flurry of activity—meetings and more meetings, phone calls, checks and double-checks. It was essential for all the players to be coordinated and in place. In addition to which, Mia was entrenched in the planning details from catering to décor and entertainment. But what made it all go down easy was that she was still floating on cloud nine from her long getaway weekend with Steven.

Since they'd been back, something was different between them. They seemed to have bonded on an entirely new level. And, oh, it was so very sweet. At times, instead of working, she found herself daydreaming about Steven and longing for the life she knew they could have together—and seemed to be working toward.

Finally, the night arrived. Michael had given Traci a set of keys so that she and Mia could drive up early to do a walk-through. This gave them the perfect opportunity to plant several listening devices throughout the house, as well as hiding two minicameras in the oversize vase of flowers that sat on a glass table facing the door.

Ashley, equipped with a telephoto lens, was stationed in a parked car just outside the property on the main road, with perfect access to the comings and goings of Michael's house. She'd already wired the ten suites at the resort, saying to Leon that she was doing a last-minute check on the accommodations. They weren't taking any chances that they would miss an incriminating conversation.

Savannah arrived under the pretext of being an additional member of Mia's team—which, of course, she really was.

Michael arrived just before six.

Mia's heart thundered in her chest. Tonight was the last opportunity she might have to bring this awful episode to a conclusion, and there was no room for error, sweet talk or tainted memories.

"Michael," she greeted him warmly. "We were just going over last-minute details. The caterer is here and the band is setting up in the back."

He took a look around, nodding his head. "Everything looks great."

"I'm sure your guests will be pleased. Oh, I wanted to introduce you to Savannah Fields." She turned to Savannah. "Savannah, this is our host, Michael Burke."

"Great to meet you," she said, shaking his hand. "I've read wonderful things about you."

"You look familiar."

Savannah smiled. "I was at the red-carpet event for Raven."

"Ahh, yes. I never forget a face."

"Savannah often helps out when I put together events. She's a whiz with details."

"Glad to have you here. I hope that you'll have some time to enjoy yourself tonight."

"I'm sure I will." She turned to Mia. "I'm going to check on the caterers and make sure they're ready as soon as the first guest walks in."

"Which should be soon," Michael said.

"Then I'd better get on it. Excuse me." She headed toward the kitchen, leaving Mia and Michael alone.

"I'm hoping that when all the dust settles with this shindig we can get together without business on the table between us. I made a promise to you and I intend to keep it."

She couldn't risk alienating him now. Not with so much at stake. "Fine. We'll talk."

He smiled, that old familiar smile, but it also held something more than familiarity. It seemed to radiate relief.

The doorbell rang, signaling the arrival of the first guest.

"Showtime," Mia said, thankful for a reason to get away.

One by one the guests arrived. Mia recognized a number of the women from the red-carpet event several weeks earlier. Danielle came in with Michelle and they quickly began to mingle with the guests.

Nick had convinced Danielle to let him help out, and when she proposed the idea to Mia, Mia decided that he would be perfect to act as valet. In that capacity he was to put tracking devices on all the women's cars.

The evening wore on and the crowd grew livelier, filled with food and plenty of good liquor. The party atmosphere was in full swing. As they grew more relaxed, the couples began pairing off. Some went upstairs, while others headed for the suites at the resort.

Danielle, realizing that the clock was ticking, knew that she had to get out of there before she got squired away by one of the male guests. Fortunately, as in most cases, there were at least two women for every man. When she excused herself from a mind-numbing conversation with a Wall Street exec who was bending her ear about stocks and bonds, she slipped outside and made a beeline for her car, waving to Ashley as she steered out onto the road. She pulled the mini-mic loose from the clip on her dress and tucked it inside her purse.

It was nearly 2:00 a.m. by the time the last guest left the house. The caterers were packing up and Mia, Savannah and Traci subtly removed the cameras and recording devices as they went from room to room, putting everything back in order.

Michael was reclining on the couch, nursing the last of his drink with a very self-satisfied look on his face. "Fabulous event."

"Thank you," Mia said. "I had good help."

He pushed up from his chair, took a white envelope from the breast pocket of his suit and handed it to Mia. "The balance for tonight."

She lifted her chin and wondered how many other women were being paid off tonight for their services. "Thanks." She tucked it in her purse. "Well," she breathed, "we need to get back." She turned for the door.

"I'll call you next week…to talk about what I mentioned."

"Sure." All she wanted to do right then was run as fast as she could into Steven's arms and put this night and all that had led up to it away for good.

The following morning, Mia contacted each of the team members to give them instructions on when and how to transfer all their information. The audio and videotapes were damning. There was no way that anyone involved would walk away scot-free. But until all the information was compiled and reviewed, it was still anyone's guess.

All the surveillance information was uploaded to Jasmine's computer at the brownstone, where she would sort and organize it before presenting it to Jean.

Their job was done, Mia thought as she sent her final transmission. Now the waiting began. But until then she could sure use the company of her girlfriends.

Everyone seemed to be talking at once. The drinks flowed and fingers were sticky with hot sauce from their favorite appetizer—buffalo wings.

Unexpected snow had begun to fall so Mia, Ashley, Danielle, Savannah and Traci enjoyed being able to huddle together.

"We did it, y'all," Danielle said, raising a wing to her lips. "I thought for sure I was gonna have to get physical with that guy who kept telling me he had someplace 'really nice' he wanted to take me."

"Oh, you mean, Congressman Stanley?" Traci asked with a smile.

"Yeah, him." She shivered, remembering.

"I got an early report from Jasmine on some of the women," Mia said.

Everyone leaned forward.

"Y'all will never guess in a zillion years who they are."

"Who?" they all asked at once, causing a few heads to turn.

Mia lowered her voice. "Housewives from Long Island. And the ringleader is the PTA president."

They all erupted in fits of laughter.

"Well, if it's not Wisteria Lane!" Ashley said.

"Yeah, some truly desperate housewives," Savannah added.

Danielle suddenly tapped her water glass with her fork. She made a big deal about clearing her throat. "I have an announcement to make."

All eyes were on her.

"Nick and I finally set the date!" Her face lit up and a big old Kool-Aid smile widened her lush mouth.

"Oh, my goodness."

"Hallelujah!"

"'Bout time that man finally made an honest woman out of you."

Danielle shook with laughter. "I'm trying to tell ya."

"So when is the big day?" ever-practical Mia asked.

"Second week in January."

Mia's eyes widened. "Hey, how about a double wedding? Claudia and Bernard were talking about December, but what if I did both of them in January?" She looked from one face to the other. Before anyone could react, Savannah had her mother on the phone, telling her the plan.

"She loves it!" Savannah said after disconnecting the call.

"Well, I will definitely have my work cut out for me," Mia said. "But this is the kind of work I'm going to love doing." She leaned over and hugged Danielle tight. "I'm so happy for you, girl."

Uncharacteristic tears filled Danielle's eyes. "I'm really happy, y'all. I'm really getting married."

"Now that deserves a toast," Ashley said.

They all raised their glasses.

"To Danielle and Nick."

"To finding true love."

"To great sex."

"To girlfriends."

They all touched glasses.

"Well, ladies, we done good," Savannah said as they prepared to leave.

"I wonder what the next assignment will be," Danielle asked, slipping into her coat.

Ashley stood and stretched. "Knowing Jean, I'm sure she'll find something to put us to the test."

They raised their empty glasses and toasted to that.

Chapter 26

Mia, always looking for a novel way to throw a party, had planned a dual bachelor and bachelorette party for Claudia and Bernard and Danielle and Nick. She didn't spare any expense when it came to food and decorations and had worked all day with the help of Ashley and Traci to ensure that everything was absolutely perfect when the guests arrived. She'd even hired a bartender and a waitress so that she and Steven could enjoy the festivities.

The party was to officially start at seven and by seven-fifteen their two-bedroom condo was packed like a night-club. Savannah and Blake came first and brought Mikayla, to everyone's delight. Bernard had invited the ladies from the health spa along with each one's significant other—Ann Marie and Sterling, Stephanie and Tony, and Elizabeth and Ron—all of whom felt like part of the family from the moment they came through the door, loaded down with gifts.

Champagne flowed, laughter filled the air and the feeling of love and affection was contagious.

Over the sound of music and animated conversation, Mia darted into the kitchen to answer the phone.

"Turn on your television."

"Jean?"

"I think you'll like what you see."

She hung up the phone and returned to the living room. While everyone else was occupied, she turned on the television to CNN. Breaking News was the banner across the screen.

A reporter was standing in front of a house in Hempstead, Long Island. Police were bringing out a woman in handcuffs. Mia gasped. It was one of the women from the party.

Savannah sidled up beside her and her mouth dropped open as the reporter went on to explain that a major escort ring has just been broken, with many of the alleged escorts being wives and mothers in this small suburban community.

By this time everyone in the room was focused on the television screen.

"Turn up the volume," Claudia said.

The picture switched to a house that Mia immediately recognized as Michael's home on Sag Harbor. Her stomach seesawed.

"Initial reports indicate that many of the customers hold political office. Warrants have been issued, although the names of the accused have not been released to the media. According to the attorney general, this is the biggest sting operation in New York City history. We will keep you posted as more information becomes available."

Mia hid the tide of emotions that rolled in her stomach. This was the man she'd once loved, and had tossed aside all her convictions of right and wrong to be with him. But he was not the man that she thought she once loved. Michael was a man who lived for the next deal, the money, and didn't care who he used to get what he wanted. It had taken this case and finding out who he really was for her to once and for all put a period at the end of their relationship. She may never know what it was he wanted to tell her and it didn't matter. It was over and she was glad she'd been the one to bring it to an end.

A ripple of "wow" undulated through the room before they each shook off the effects of what they'd just seen and returned to party mode.

The girls, including Claudia, slipped into the kitchen unnoticed.

"To success, ladies," Mia said, looking from one to the other. "I couldn't have done it without each one of you." She raised an empty glass in mock salute.

"What are you ladies celebrating?"

"Just girl stuff," Mia said, sliding her arm around her man's waist.

"Well, I have something to celebrate, too."

"What?"

He took Mia by the hand. "Come on and I'll show you." He ushered her back into the living room, with all her friends trailing behind.

"Excuse me, ladies and gentlemen," Steven shouted over the music and laughter.

Blake crossed the room and lowered the music.

"Since this is a day of celebrations for two of my favorite couples—" he turned to Mia "—I want to celebrate the rest of my life with you."

A soft gasp of expectation filled the room.

"I want to come home to you, sleep and wake with you. Share my joys and sorrows with you." He reached into his pants pocket and took out a diamond ring set in platinum with tiny diamonds encrusted on the band.

Mia began to shake.

"You're my world."

"You go, boy!" Blake cheered.

Mia's eyes filled.

"Say you'll marry me and finally make me complete."

For a moment she couldn't breathe, she couldn't think. It all seemed so surreal. And when she looked into his eyes, saw the depth of his feelings for her hovering there, the dam finally broke.

"Yes, yes, yes, I'll marry you."

Whoops of joy exploded in the room.

Steven put the ring on her finger and gathered her up in his embrace. "I love you," he said for her ears only. "I love you," he repeated.

Her heart swelled to bursting and tears spilled from her eyes. This was joy, Mia thought. This was true happiness. One man devoted to one woman, wanting only each other and the best for each other. This was love. The real thing, and she was never going to let it go.

They kissed as if they were the only two people in the room. And to them they were.

Can he overcome the past to fight for the future…?

Favorite author

YAHRAH ST. JOHN

THIS TIME *for* REAL

For years, widow Peyton Sawyer has avoided romance…
until, volunteering at the community center, she
experiences an immediate smoldering connection
with director Malik Williams. But Malik is haunted
by the past and doesn't think he can give Peyton the
relationship he knows she deserves.

"St. John has done a fantastic job with her debut
release."—*Romantic Times BOOKreviews*
on *ONE MAGIC MOMENT*

*Available the first week of February 2009
wherever books are sold.*

KIMANI™
ROMANCE

It's a complicated road from friendship to love...

Favorite author

Ann Christopher

Road to Seduction

Eric and Isabella have been best friends forever—until
now. When a road trip unleashes serious sexual tension,
Izzy's afraid falling for playboy Eric is a sure path to
heartache. And Eric's scared of ruining their cherished
friendship. Friends or lovers? They're tempted to find out.

"Christopher has a gift for storytelling."
—Romantic Times BOOKreviews

*Available the first week of February 2009
wherever books are sold.*

KIMANI
ROMANCE ™

Discovering the love of a lifetime...

NEW YORK TIMES BESTSELLING AUTHOR

BRENDA JACKSON

SECRET LOVE

A Madaris Family Novel

When celebrity actress Diamond Swain comes to
Whispering Pines—a remote Texas ranch—to hide from
the paparazzi, she instantly finds herself at odds with
owner Jake Madaris. Jake doesn't have time to babysit
some Hollywood star, yet he finds himself drawn into a
whirlwind secret romance. But is what he shares with her
strong enough to overcome the media's prying eyes?

"Jackson turns up the heat...with her special
brand of intrigue."—*Rendezvous*

*Available the first week of February 2009
wherever books are sold.*

ARABESQUE®

www.kimanipress.com
www.myspace.com/kimanipress

KPBJI200209

ESSENCE Bestselling Author

DONNA HILL

SEX AND LIES

Book 1 of the new T.L.C. miniseries

Their job hawking body products for Tender Loving Care
is a cover for their true identities as undercover operatives for
a covert organization. And when Savannah Fields investigates
a case of corporate espionage, the trail of corruption leads
right back to her husband!

Coming the first week of February wherever books are sold.

KIMANI™
ROMANCE

www.kimanipress.com   KPDH0520208

Should she believe the facts?

Essence bestselling author

DONNA HILL

SEDUCTION AND LIES

Book 2 of the TLC miniseries

Hawking body products for Tender Loving Care is just a cover. The real deal? They're undercover operatives for a covert organization. Newest member Danielle Holloway's first assignment is to infiltrate an identity-theft ring. But when the clues lead to her charismatic beau, Nick Mateo, Danielle has more problems than she thought.

TLC—There's more to these ladies than Tender Loving Care!

Coming the first week of December wherever books are sold.